Banyon

Terrell L Bowers

Copyright © 2012 Author Name

All rights reserved.

ISBN:1539800105
ISBN-13:9781539800101

DEDICATION

For Rita Brenig, my first editor. She worked with me to help turn my stories and characters into Western novels.

Chapter One

After five years as a deputy U.S. Marshal, Mace Banyon was out of a job. Well, he had lost that particular job ... using excessive force, during the apprehension of several dangerous killers. Funny how everyone was happy to see those men dead or behind bars, but then some naïve moron lawyer charged that Mace had acted out of vengeance on the last case. A softhearted – albeit more a case of *soft-headed* – Judge had agreed, and Mace was stripped of his badge and position.

The perpetrator in question had a reputation for violence, having been locked up on a number of occasions. But this time, he had kidnapped a seven-year-old girl, terrorized her for over a week, while keeping her in a fruit cellar like an animal, nearly starving the poor child to death. When his ransom turned out to be a sack of straw, he had vowed to kill the little girl. Mace had done his job. Before the kidnapper could make good his threat, Mace allowed him the chance to grab for his gun. A bullet in his brain had ended the episode and Mace had returned the unfortunate tyke to her grateful parents.

Mace let out a short sigh, having just finished breakfast at a cafe. He couldn't really blame the judge, for the outcry of the newspaper was prompted by the single jack-leg lawyer – who mostly wanted some publicity – and decried how the stinking, pervert kidnapper had civil rights. In retrospect, he shouldn't have shot the human maggot in the head. It had the look of an execution, rather than self-defense. The fuss made little sense – the child-napper would have been hanged for his crime. Given the same choice, Mace would prefer a bullet and quick death, rather than a public hanging.

With the skewed thinking of people like the lawyer and the newspaper man, one day soon, criminals would be given nothing but sympathy and understanding, while their victims would get nothing but grief and heartache!

Shoving those thoughts to the back of his mind, he looked forward to his new job. Silas Temple represented a land corporation back East, and he had been in the courtroom for Mace Banyon's hearing. He wasted no time offering the ex-deputy marshal a job in Oasis, California supervising tenant farmers and collecting fees that were due the company. It sounded like a peaceful, rocking-chair position.

Having arrived late last night in Oasis, Mace looked forward to riding out to the fine house provided and meet with a man named Tincup Kelly, who was to be his foreman. He paid for his meal and stepped out to get a look at his new hometown.

There was a wide main street, with a long row of buildings to either side. On a secondary street, there were numerous homes and a section that appeared to be exclusively Chinese. Coming from Kansas, Mace had encountered a few Chinese, and found them inoffensive. In fact, he'd never seen a warrant on a Chinese person, not for any crime whatsoever.

He was impressed with the full array of businesses: a freight and telegraph office, hotels, rooming houses, two saloons, a dozen shops and stores, a huge stable, a bank, and even a jail. He started toward the livery when a ruckus broke out up the street.

A dark-haired girl in a cotton jacket and pants was struggling with three men. A fourth man had come to her defense and was yelling at the trio. Upon closer inspection, Mace could see the girl was Chinese. He glanced at the Sheriff's office, but there was no sign of life.

He didn't intend to get involved in a fight that was not his concern, for he no longer carried a bade. But it wouldn't hurt to see that any fight remained fair.

Approaching unheeded by the men in the street, Mace stopped in front of Kemph's General Store, standing next to a display of rakes, shovels, picks and a variety of tools.

'Ain't none of your affair!' the biggest man of the trio was warning the solitary man who had squared off against the trio. Mace noted the lone gent was smaller and considerably older than any of the three he faced.

'And I'm warning you, Bruno,' the little man shot back, 'you touch one hair on that gal's head, and I'll dance on your grave before sundown!'

It was strong talk for a man without a gun, and Mace felt admiration for his courage. There he stood, alone, with three bigger men facing him, and he was the one doing the threatening. It was foolhardy, but it showed he had grit.

The girl twisted in the arms of one of the three, the youngest. He appeared to be drunk, though it was early in the day. His eyes were red, and he was almost overwhelmed by the girl's strength, even though he was half-again her size.

'Please...' she begged. 'Please let me go!'

Bruno spun on the girl snarling with hate and malice in his expression.

'Shut you're rice chute sweetie!' he sneered. 'We are being friendly with your kind. If you refuse us a kiss, we'll just have to pin you to the ground and take what we want!'

'You asked for it!' the little man snapped, raising his fists. 'You've been pushing us around long enough, Bruno. Well, it's time someone put you in your place!'

Bruno's neck was as thick as a bull's, and his unkempt red hair and pig-black eyes added to a look of ferocity. He raised his own meaty paws – both the size of cannonballs, and started towards the smaller man.

'No! Tincup!' the girl screamed. 'Don't!'

Mace groaned. *Tincup?* The little fellow about to get his head handed to him in a bucket was Tincup? *His* Tincup Kelly?

Mace couldn't believe it. *Silas Temple! You underhanded sneak! Is this why you hired me? To came down here to fight a war?*

Tincup lashed out with a jab, smacking Bruno in the face. It was the only punch he landed. Bruno took charge at once, knocking Tincup sideways with one punch, then pummeling him with two or three shots. The last blow to his jaw sent the man sprawling.

Bruno laughed, nodded to the young man holding the girl, and held out his hands. 'A little inspiration is what I need, Rodney. Give her to me!'

Rodney swung the girl in his direction and gave her a push. Bruno grabbed her arms with his large hands, and drew her close, forcing a kiss.

Mace felt his hackles rise. What was wrong with these people? No one was saying or doing anything to stop this bullying! A man was beaten and a woman was being assaulted on the main street of town!

'My turn!' the third man guffawed licentiously. 'Give Renz a turn!'

Bruno threw her into Renz's arms. The man also stole a hasty kiss and threw her back to Rodney. Meanwhile, Tincup was on his hands and knees, spitting a mouthful of blood into the dirt. He was summoning enough strength to stand.

Bruno glared at the man. 'Get up, Kelly!' he roared. 'Come and dance on my grave!'

Mace had seen enough. He couldn't stand by and do nothing. The man on the ground was his employee ... or would be. And no woman should be humiliated and molested like that, especially in public!

He selected an item from the tool rack and stepped forward.

'Hey, pig-face!' Mace challenged to Bruno's back.

The brute had doubled his fists, ready to deal out more punishment to the over-matched, and not yet on his feet, Tincup Kelly. He swung around to see who dared call him a name--

The pick handle smacked him solidly between the eyes! Bruno's head jerked back from the blow and his body recoiled too fast for his feet to keep up. The result – he landed flat on his back in the middle of the street, arms twitching like a fish out of water. His mouth worked, but he couldn't collect his wits. He lay there staring up at the morning sky, eyes glazed and a lax expression on his face.

Mace surveyed the onlookers, ready to strike again if necessary. Most of them backed away, not wanting any part of a man wielding a club. When his gaze rested on Renz, he experienced a familiar emotion. Within the man's eyes was the same look he had seen a number of times, and each time he had been forced to kill or be killed himself.

Renz studied Mace with a curious gaze, his eyes a pale blue, as inanimate as those of a snake. Mace sensed a deadly warning written in their depths and watched for his reaction.

'Who are you, tough guy?' Renz asked, his hand resting next to his low-slung gun.

Mace had the handle in his left hand, allowing his right to dangle near his own gun. The precaution was not wasted on the gunman.

'I'm nobody special,' he answered casually. 'But I take exception to anyone who molests a young lady.'

'Bruno will kill you when he comes to,' Renz warned. 'If I were you, I'd head for some far-off place ... Mexico comes to mind.'

Mace grinned. 'I don't intend to learn Spanish, but thanks for the warning.' Then he put a cool look on Rodney, the man holding the girl. 'You can either let her go now, or end up lying on the ground next to Bruno .... your choice.'

Rodney cast a nervous glance at Renz. The gunman nodded, so he released the girl. She immediately dropped to her knees next to Kelly, tending to his injuries.

Mace had experience with crowds, so he looked around. 'Unless you people get a special enjoyment out of watching men bleed, I suggest one of you find the town doctor.' With a wary look at Renz, 'I think the excitement is over for the time being.'

The people began to disperse, but a few of them stopped as a new man appeared on the scene. He had a star pinned to his vest.

'What's going on here?' he demanded to know in a gruff voice. He came to a stop, his eyes flicking from Mace to the pick handle in his hand, to the two men on the ground.

'Renz, what happened?'

The cold-eyed man shrugged. 'We was having a little harmless fun with the young lady. Tincup took exception and Bruno convinced him to mind his own business. Then this jasper decided to take a hand. He about knocked Bruno's head off'n his shoulders. Didn't give him any warning at all, just clouted him when he wasn't looking.'

'That right, stranger?' the sheriff asked, frowning.

'If you take a closer look, I did hit Bruno in the face, so, in point of fact, he *was* looking at me.'

'You getting smart with me?' the lawman growled.

'No, Sheriff, I haven't enough time for you to catch up.' As the badge was trying to decide if that was an insult, Mace said, 'There seemed to be a dispute over whether this young lady could walk freely on the street without being accosted.'

'A-cost what?'

'Harassed, picked on, bullied, manhandled,' Mace explained. 'Where I come from, we don't stand idly by while men lay hands on a defenseless woman.'

'I could arrest you,' the sheriff pointed out. 'You've got no right to –

'To do what? Your job?' Mace cut him short.

The sheriff was near Banyon's age – mid- to late-twenties, and slightly thinner in build. His face darkened at Mace being so quick to exercise wit and insults.

'I don't need no club-wielding son to come into my town and tell me my job.'

Mace said, 'Good. Then we are in agreement. You can plainly see that – short of shooting Bruno – I did the only thing I could to stop the fight and the abuse of an innocent girl.'

The sheriff looked around and saw a number of people were bobbing their heads in agreement. He hadn't been there, and Bruno might have killed Tincup Kelly. He finally simmered down and turned to Renz.

'Better get Bruno over to the doc. And, Rodney,' he added, looking at the young man who had been holding the girl, 'you'd best get out to your place. Your pa will be wondering why you didn't come home last night.'

Mace put back the wooden handle, then moved over and helped Tincup onto his feet. The man couldn't stand under his own power, so he hefted him over his shoulder. The girl stared at him in wonder.

'Where to, ma'am?' he asked.

'His dwelling is near China village,' she replied, as if that might make a difference to Mace.

'Lead the way,' he said.

The girl picked up Tincup's hat, and then hurried up the street. He couldn't help but smile, for he'd seldom seen a woman wearing cotton trousers, even beneath a rather long smock. The sash revealed that she had a slender waist, and her long braids bounced as she walked. There was a dignity and grace in her movements, despite the recent unpleasantness.

She led Mace to an alley, down between two houses, and to a small shack. It was not much to look at, with a half-hung shutter, peeling paint, and a sagging roof. Inside, there was a cot in one corner. Mace put the man down gently, surprised the girl had already rounded up a pan of water and a cloth. As he stepped back, she immediately began to dab at the blood on his face with a damp rag.

'I presume this fellow is Tincup Kelly,' he stated, looking over her shoulder.

The remark caused her to glance back at him with curious eyes. 'Yes,' she said simply, returning to the chore at hand.

'You speak good English,' he observed. 'Did you go to school here in America?'

'I was *born* in America,' she said a crisply.

Mace pulled one of two chairs away from a warped table, wishing he had not stuck his foot in his mouth. He sat down and quietly waited for the girl to finish treating the still-unconscious man. She did not turn around until she had covered him with a blanket.

'He has some bruises, but I don't think he lost any teeth and the jaw is not broken.'

'How did you and Tincup get into trouble with those three jaspers?' Mace asked.

'It was my fault,' she said quickly. 'Our own store has very limited goods. I needed several things from Kemph's market. I didn't think any of Mr Havelock's men would be around so early in the day. Tincup arrived when they stopped me in the street, and trouble started.'

'What's the relationship between you and Tincup?'

Her frown deepened. 'Relationship?'

'Yes, is he a friend, a relative, or does he simply enjoy taking a beating every now and again.'

She gazed in Tincup's direction once more. 'I have known him for many years. He even speaks a little Chinese. He is one of the few white friends we have now.'

'Now?'

Her furrowed brow showed her curiosity. 'You don't seem to be very informed about the Chinese here in Oasis. Where do you come from?'

Mace paused to remove the taste of his boots once more. He couldn't deny being ignorant about the Chinese, but it was an embarrassment to admit it.

He decided to be straight with her, 'I hail from Kansas, ma'am. I'm not much for reading newspapers and I don't listen much to general gossip. It tends to leave a few blanks when it comes to how much I've learned in my twenty-seven years of this here life. 'I apologize for not knowing much of anything about the situation here in Oasis.'

'So that is why you risk your own life to help me and Tincup,' she said with a degree of certainty. 'You don't hate us ... yet.'

It was Mace's turn to frown. 'Say what?' He shook his head. 'Why on earth would I hate you or the other Chinese?'

Her eyes lowered, looking at the floor. 'It is difficult to understand myself. I don't think I should speak of such things to a stranger.'

'Well, I might be a stranger, but I was hired to work with Tincup,' he said. 'I would think that puts me on his side of whatever issue it is you don't wish to share with me.'

She gaped at his declaration. 'You are the new land manager?'

'I was hired by the Temple Land Development Company to oversee his farms here in Oasis,' he informed her.

'Then I work for you, Mr Banyon. Many of the Chinese work for you!'

Chapter Two

After the initial surprise wore off, Banyon rented a carryall and took Tincup Kelly to his company home. Come to find out, the place was within walking distance – less than a half-mile from Oasis. From the roof of one of the buildings in town, he could have seen the place.

He was relieved to discover the Land Manager's house was quite large and had three bedrooms. Questioning the girl – she introduced herself as Su Lee – she was both housekeeper and cook, with her father maintaining the rather large garden and lawn. The groceries she had been trying to buy was so she would have American food stored in the house for his meals.

The girl's father took the team and Mace's horse to the barn. There were several other horses in the corral and he assured Mace his choice of animal would be ready anytime he needed one – day or night. He seemed eager to serve, volunteered to return the carryall to town, and bowed several times during their short conversation.

A quick survey of the land Temple controlled revealed that all of the tenant farmers were Chinese. It was also apparent that this was the prime property in the valley, as it had access to irrigation and the ground was pliable and rich, perfect for farming. Even without interviewing the people in town or in the outlying areas, it struck Mace why there would be jealousy and envy. This was obvioulsy the best farm land for miles around.

Mace looked over a journal with the account listings for each family working, along with their acreage, crops and earnings. Some were doing quite well, while others had only meager returns. In all, it was a very profitable enterprise.

'Mr Banyon,' Su Lee interrupted his study. 'You said you wanted to know when Tincup was awake.' He looked up and she added: 'I gave him some of his ... tonic, and he is much improved.'

Mace guessed the tonic was alcohol, thanked her for calling him, and accompanied her to the guest room. Tincup was sitting up, glaring at a bowl of broth Su Lee had given him.

'What's your thinkin', Su Lee?' he barked the question. 'I only got hit once or twice. I can still eat real food.'

'I will prepare you a meal when Mr Banyon is ready to eat ... not before,' she informed him curtly. 'The broth will help to settle your stomach from drinking hard liquor so early in the day.'

He didn't reply to her, but looked at Mace. A haggard smile lit up the elderly man's face.

'Su tells me we met in town – whilst I was nappin' in the middle of the street.'

'Got to hand it to you,' Mace said. 'You picked the biggest man to fight with that I've seen in the last three hundred miles.'

'Always had more spunk than ability,' he said, fingering the bruise on the side of his jaw. 'That Bruno put me down and out before I could even show him my fancy footwork. I used to do a little boxing years back.'

'Was that before the war or before gun powder was invented?' Mace sallied.

The old man snorted, Su Lee left the two men alone, and Mace straddle the only room's only chair.

'Time to get serious, old-timer,' he began. 'It appears to me that Silas Temple left out a few details about my new job. Maybe you could fill me in.'

'Whatever you want to know,' he offered.

'First off, what all does my job entail? I was told my primary chore would be to keep a ledger, collect rent after the sale of crops, that sort of thing.'

Tincup snickered. 'You're 'bout as green as I was when I joined my first gold rush, back in '49. Me and about a hundred thousand other people went searching. Out of that number, I think there were six or seven who actually found enough gold to brag about it. The rest of us starved. I would have, 'ceptin' I began collecting assorted pans and pots. I used to have tin cups dangling from my mule's mane – earned me the nickname. I liked it better than Clarence and kept it.'

'How'd you end up here in Oasis?'

'I worked for a mining company for a time, hired out with some Chinese. We got a portion of what we dug out or panned. After a year or so, the gold petered out. Old Tong Hing Lee and I became good friends, so we packed up and went to work on the railroad.' He made a face. 'That was a cold, miserable, back-breaking job.'

He took a spoonful of broth and shook his head. 'Man can't live on this stuff.' He snickered at his own statement. 'But I reckon the Chinese could. Never saw men work so hard and eat so little. Rice and dried fish ... ugh!'

'And how did you end up here?'

'We both worked for Temple, during a time when he had been contracted to lay sections of rail, but the jobs petered out once the main lines were finished. He mentioned he had found several tracts of good farm land and suggested I get some of my friends and come to work. There wasn't a lot of options when the economy crashed. Plus, many of these Chinese had lived on farms before they migrated to America.

'The Paxton place was the only one around who had bothered to dig wells and put in a couple ditches for irrigation. The rest of the farms were available cheap, because there had been news about a new gold strike in Colorado. Temple took advantage and bought most of the valley.'

'And he made you foreman?'

'Yeah, but I never learn't to read or write, and when I get more than ten dollars, I can't keep track of my money. I told him I'd do the leg work, but I had to have help to run the business. Temple sent a man from back East to handle the books and I got Tong Lee to bring his friends and build on the different sections. Next thing, we were in business, selling produce and shipping it to the rail-head.'

'So what went wrong? How come there's so much dislike for the Chinese?'

'You been listening, son? Best land and water for a hundred miles around, hard-working people – every late-comer, dry farmer in the valley envies us.'

'And the last manager? What happened to him?'

'Uh, well, he didn't exactly have the innards for dealing with conflict, if you know what I mean.'

'He was yellow.'

Tincup chuckled. 'As a ripe banana.'

'How much of the trouble is words and intimidation, compare to actual acts of violence?'

'We've had some threats, some cattle driven over a field, and the occasional beating or manhandling -- like today with Su Lee. So far no one has been killed.'

'Where does the sheriff stand?' Mace asked.

'Ace Wilcox has been trying real hard to ride the fence, but you know how uncomfortable that can get. He's being pressured to side against us by Seth Havelock, the biggest bear in these here woods. You met two of his men today – Bruno and Renz.'

'Havelock have a ranch or farm of his own?'

'No, he's mostly a banker with an appetite for money. As for hired mutts, he has the two you met and a man named Whitey Curn … a tough customer with a gun.'

'I'd think a banker would be happy to have farms that made their mortgage on time. Why does he want the land?'

'Temple owns these farms – no mortgage payments. As for the banker,' Tincup did not hide his contempt, 'I've heard he was one of those carpetbaggers after the war. Made a pile of money on other people's grief and loss, then came to California to double his fortune. If he can force us and the Chinese to abandon this valley, he can swoop in and buy the place from Temple for pennies on the dollar. He could get rich.'

'I might have to do a little banking,' Mace said. 'Could be the man will listen to reason.'

'A waste of your breath, Banyon. Havelock is a very determined man.'

Mace grinned. 'I've been known to be determined myself a time or two.'

The old boy's face cracked into a smile. 'I reckon you might have at that. I mean, why else would Temple have picked your for the job?'

Mace laughed, thinking, *Why else indeed!*

Su Lee opened the door a crack. Seeing that both Mace and Tincup were momentarily silent, she pushed it a bit wider. She bowed slightly.

'A man to see you, Mr Banyon. It is the sheriff.'

Mace told Tincup to get some rest, suggesting he put off any work till the next morning, then followed the girl into the hallway. She paused to look at him.

'I was about to prepare your evening meal. Will you be long?'

'I doubt it, but you and your father can start without me.'

She lifted her eyebrows. 'We do not eat with the plantation manager.'

'Why not?'

'You are the master of the house and overseer of all of the farms. It would not be proper for us to sit at the same table. Father would not hear of it.'

'And you? What's your objection?'

'Until I marry, I am not permitted to eat at a table other than my family's. After I wed, I shall eat only at the table of my husband.'

'And that's what, a Chinese code of conduct?'

'Father is very traditional and it is our heritage, Mr Banyon. Please don't ask us to change. It would be impossible.'

'You said you were born here; you are an American,' he stated. 'I should think you could choose your own future and the rules you wish to live by.'

'I honor my father's wishes,' she said patiently.

'OK,' he let the matter drop. 'I doubt the sheriff and I will be more than a few minutes.'

She gave a nod and disappeared. Mace went into the front room to meet Ace Wilcox, wondering what the man had to say.

Wilcox stood awkwardly in a corner of the room, hat in his hands. He straightened as Mace entered.

'Howdy, Sheriff,' Mace greeted him. 'I didn't expect to see you again today.'

'You might have told me who your were, Banyon.'

'Would my name have meant that much to you?'

The sheriff glowered. 'You know what I mean. We've had word you were coming since late last week.'

'I didn't know I rated all that much attention.'

'You aiming to cause trouble? Is that why you accepted the job?'

'I was hired to mange a group of tenant farmers, Sheriff. Silas Temple didn't tell me about any trouble here in your valley. I thought this would be a cushy job, sitting around, getting fat, and stuffing money in a bank account for my retirement years.'

'You didn't waste time causing trouble.'

'Stick to the facts, Sheriff,' Mace told him sharply. 'I knew I was supposed to work with a man name Tincup Kelly. Letting that big ape beat him to death would have left me without a clue as to what my job was or how to do it.'

'So you started out your duties by blind-siding the meanest man in town!'

'I don't worry about fighting fair when my opponent is twice my size. If Bruno comes after me, I'll be looking for another weapon to equal the contest.'

'The problem is, Banyon, you've been in town less than a day and you've already made an enemy of the most powerful man in town.'

'Well,' Mace remained defensive, 'Tincup tells me that was a foregone conclusion, before I even hit town. I don't worry about getting off on the wrong foot, when I'm not invited to a dance. But when the music starts, I know how to kick up my heels.'

Wilcox cracked a smile. 'You've got a long-winded way of saying you aren't going to avoid a fight.'

'If you know my name, you likely know my reputation, Sheriff.' Mace outlined. 'When I get pushed, I push back – hard!'

The man studied Mace for a few seconds. 'You don't look like a cold, calculating killer.'

'I used my gun in the line of duty, Sheriff. I never shot a man who wasn't in the process of trying to shoot me.' He paused and added: 'Although I admit, I did encourage the last man I put in the ground to go for his gun. Anyone who hurts or kidnaps women or children ... I have no problem making them pay.'

'I hear you,' he said in accord.

'And,' Mace waved his hand in the direction of the numerous farms under his contract, 'several of these farmers have wives and children. I won't hold with anyone doing harm to them or their livelihood.'

The sheriff didn't appear happy with the statement, but he let it stand. He turned for the door and stopped, looking over his shoulder.

'Try to keep a handle on your people, when they come into town. They are safer when they stay in the Chinese area. If they cross into the main business district ... well, Havelock's men are watching for any chance to pick on them.'

'I'll do what I can,' Mace said. 'On the other hand, it's up to you to discourage any of those troublemakers from coming out here. I don't need to remind you, these people might look and dress differently, but they are Americans.'

He grunted. 'I know that better than you might think. Su Lee and a few of the others working out here were born in this country. I didn't arrive in America until I was five years old.'

'Thanks for the visit, Sheriff,' Mace ended the visit.

Donning his hat, Wilcox went out the door. The man seemed to have a good heart, but he wore his gun like a job requirement, with the holster twisted around until it was up almost over his back pocket. Plus, it didn't look to have a tie-down lace to hitch around the thigh to keep it in place. When he walked, it was not the fluid, cat-like moves of a fighter, but clumsy and slow. If it came to a battle, Wilcox would not be much help.

Mace had a quick lonely meal, then strapped on his gun, put on his hat, and went out to find himself a horse.

No sooner was he out the door than Tong Hing Lee appeared.

'I have a horse ready, but I can get a team for the buckboard, if you prefer.'

'Dad-gum, Mr Lee! What made you think I'd be going for a ride this late?'

'My job: be ready all'a time,' he said, as a matter-of-fact. 'I keep horse with saddle all'a time you awake. Then, before you wake in morning, Tong have horse ready.'

'You deserve a raise, my friend,' he told him. 'If you can give me directions to Havelock's house, I'll see you get one.'

***

The Havelock place resembled a plantation mansion, with huge pillars supporting a large porch roof, along with several outbuildings, including a barn and attached carriage house. There were two buggies, and three horses moving about in a nearby corral.

Mace dismounted at the front of the house and used the hitch rail to tie-off his horse. Then he walked up to massive twin-doors, easily ten-foot tall, and used an engraved door-knocker to bang against the skillfully stained wood. He waited a moment, then knocked a second time.

The door opened to reveal a pretty young woman, possibly still in her teens. She wore a simple but expensive dress, her hair was piled neatly atop her head, and he caught a whiff of flowery perfume. She appraised Mace with a curious gleam in her eyes.

'May I be of service to you?' she asked politely.

'I'd like a few words with Seth Havelock,' he informed her. 'Is he your father?'

The girl threw an anxious look over her slender shoulder and, instead of inviting him in, stepped out to the porch and pulled the door closed behind her.

'You're that new boss over the Chinese farmers, aren't you?'

He gave an affirmative nod. 'I work for the Temple Land Development Company.'

She wrinkled her brow. 'Why do you wish to see my husband?'

Mace was stunned. 'You're *Mrs Havelock?* The banker's *wife?*'

Her dark expression did not change. 'Seth is my husband.' Her words held no warmth.

'Pardon me for saying so, but you look a mite young,' he was candid. 'Somehow, I expected Havelock to be a calculating, bitter old bachelor, whose only mistress was his money.'

She appeared to relax. 'Close. But you left out icy-cold, unfeeling and completely ruthless.'

'With all those fine qualities,' he was sarcastic, 'It's easy to understand why most any woman would be proud to be his wife.'

She lifted a shoulder and let it fall. 'My family had a farm, a fairly comfortable house, and several kids to raise. I was the price my father was willing to pay to save our place after a fire destroyed our crops.'

'He bartered you to Havelock?'

'I'm certain Seth was behind the *accidental* fire.' Another shrug. 'It doesn't matter. It was either Seth or a forty-year-old neighbor who had an orchard. Seth made the better offer, so here I am. There's little use in complaining.'

'Yet you told me,' he reminded her, 'a complete stranger.'

'Not exactly a stranger, Mr Banyon.' The wisp of a smile passed across her lips. 'Your name has been on my husband's lips since we got word Mr Temple had hired a replacement. The last manager was run off within a month.'

'I'm surprised Seth confides in you.'

She uttered a feminine grunt. 'Not really. I often overhear him talking to his flunkies and, when he drinks, he swears oaths about you.' Another grunt. 'He drinks a lot ... more since he learned who you were.'

'Nice to know the telegraph service is so up to date in Oasis.'

'After clouting Bruno today, you are sure to remain Seth's number one subject.'

Mace looked past her to the closed door. 'Are you preventing me from talking to your husband for a reason?'

'Talking to him will do no good. Seth is determined to own this valley, especially the rich farm land your employees are on.'

'They are tenant farmers, not employees,' he corrected. 'In time, each of them will own the land they are working.'

She smiled at him as if he was dull-witted. 'Seth will never let you succeed. He will do whatever it takes to stop you.'

'If he goes too far, then he and I will share more than words.'

Mrs Havelock decided Mace was not going to leave without seeing Seth. She reopened the door and spoke loudly enough for her voice to be heard from inside the big house.

'Won't you come in, Mr Banyon. I'll tell my husband that you're here.'

Mace followed her into a large sitting room. He looked around slowly, noting the lush carpeting and expensive leather-covered couch, chairs and divan. There were several portraits of important-looking men about the room, including a staunch-pose of General Lee in his dress Yankee uniform.

Banyon turned his attention back to the hallway, where a man had suddenly appeared. He was fairly large, but not heavyset. He had a dollar-cigar between his teeth and scrutinized Mace with probing dark eyes. He entered the room with an air of authority, suchlike a general himself, inspecting one of his subordinate officers. He stopped three feet from Mace, nearly even in height at a couple inches under six feet, although a few pounds heavier. For a banker, he was built sturdy and tough.

Removing his cigar with yellow-stained fingers, he spit a piece of tobacco from the tip of his tongue. He ignored the fact it landed somewhere on his expensive flooring.

'So you're Mace Banyon, huh?'

'Unless my mother lied to me all those years.'

He grunted sourly at the attempted humor. 'You don't look so tough. I guess that's why you used a club on Bruno.'

'It won't hurt his malicious features. It looks as if someone beat him with an ugly club years ago.'

'Why did you interfere in a simple fight between two men?'

'Bruno had won the fight and was getting a little carried away,' Mace said. 'I thought he deserved to be carried away himself.'

'You've a sass about you, but you talk like an educated man. Maybe we can make some kind of arrangement between us.'

'The only arrangement I'm interested in is you keeping your dogs on a leash. I don't want them harassing my farmers.'

'Those farmers have something I want,' he acknowledged bluntly. 'Being Chinese, they don't have the support of many of the people in the valley. That puts you all by yourself.'

'Chinese, white, Mexican or Indian, Havelock,' Mace said, regarding the man with a frosty stare, 'if they are working one of my farms, they are under my protection.'

'You've taken a hand in high-stakes poker, with only one chip to your name, Banyon. I own the casino, the table, the dealer, and the deck is staked against you. I don't see you winning enough to stay in the game.'

'Lady Luck sometimes smiles on the man down to his last chip.'

Havelock snorted. ' Not this time, Banyon. You ain't got a prayer.'

Mace smiled his widest smirk. 'A man who's in the right has always got a prayer, Havelock ... and sometimes the answer is Yes!'

Without waiting for the man's response, Mace spun on his heel and went out of the massive doors. Back on his horse, he heaved a sigh. As long as he could remember, trouble had followed after him. This time, he had arrived second, because trouble was already here and waiting!

Chapter Three

After a quick breakfast with Tincup, Banyon found his already-saddled sorrel standing at the hitching post. He told Tincup to take it easy for the day and set out to look over the land and farmers who were under Temple's contracts.

Tincup had given him a good description of the land, and it was impressive. Temple had acquired three sections of land, all prime bottom land. At 640 acres to the section, it added up to three square miles of mostly irrigated ground.

Some of the workers had grown up trying to farm ground in the rocky hills of China, so this was a snap to them. With ample water and tools, they had full, high-growing fields of grain, corn, beans and a variety of other vegetables.

Mace looked at each farm in turn, spoke for a short time with the workers, and then moved on down the line. Several knew only broken English, so he kept his remarks and questions very basic. They knew who he was, for old Tong Hing Lee had made the rounds the previous day, telling of his bravery against Bruno and the other two men in town. Mace was greeted warmly at each place he visited.

Beyond the Temple boundary was the Paxton farm and, like the others along the river, it flourished. Paxton had been the one man Temple had not been able to buy out, and it was easy to see why. His place was picturesque, with a huge white ranch-style house, a massive barn and corrals, and a full gamut of livestock.

Mace waved at a man in the fields and was rewarded with a return wave. He didn't bother to ride out and visit, for the man was working earnestly with a hoe. Weeds constantly competed with the planted crops and had to be removed by hand ... a job Mace wanted no part of.

The best part of the morning was gone, so Mace neck-reined his sorrel, turning towards the main road. He crossed a small ravine, wound through some brush and trees, and hit the trail at the base of the nearest mountain range.

Pausing to rest his horse in the shade of a sprawling cedar for a few minutes, he enjoyed the peace and quiet and coolness of the air. Starting off again, he hadn't gone but a short way when he came to a shallow dell and saw a small freight wagon ahead of him. It wasn't moving and he could see no driver. Drawing closer, he ascertained someone sitting on the ground in front of one of the forward wheels, almost under the wagon tongue. It came as a shock, discovering it was a girl, and she was working furiously, pulling and tugging at something.

Finally, the girl began to unbutton the back of her dress. She had one sleeve pulled down over bare shoulder before she became aware of his presence. She sucked in her breath in surprise and jerked the sleeve back up, almost tearing it with such a violent motion.

'Beg pardon, miss,' Mace said easily. 'I didn't mean to startle you.'

She put her back against the rod shaft, still sitting with her legs folded under her, only inches from the wheel of the wagon. Her hair was dangling loosely, fine oak-colored hair that shimmered in the noonday sun. She regarded him with bright, alert, very dark-brown eyes, which set off a nicely shaped nose and mouth. There was a trace of pink from her throat and up into her cheeks from her chagrin, but she recovered her composure at once.

'I – I didn't hear you coming,' she almost apologized. 'I looked along the trail, but I did not see anyone.'

'I didn't exactly come here by way of the main road, miss.' Then looking over her situation, he could see the problem. The wheel was sitting on the bottom part of her dress, and it had her pinned to the ground.

He stopped his horse next to the back of the wagon and dismounted.

'Didn't you set the brake?' he asked, seeing the wheel was deeply seated in a rut.

'I must not have got the handle all the way locked,' she answered meekly. 'As I was climbing down from the wagon, it rolled forward into the rut. I fell against the wheel and – well, you can see – it rolled onto the hem of my dress and I was pinned.

'You're not hurt, are you?" he queried, kneeling down to take a closer look.

'No. Luckily, the wheel stopped once it dropped into the hole. I managed to get both feet out of the way.'

Mace, in spite of himself, grinned. 'So you were going to undress right here in the road, pull the team forward, then don your duds again.'

Another mortified simper, and the girl's cheeks grew more rosy.

'That won't be necessary now – not if you'll lend me a hand.'

'Be my pleasure, miss,' he volunteered.

The wheel was almost against her upper legs, so there was no way the wagon could be pulled forward, and the rut was deep. If he tried to back up the team, she might get stepped on or kicked, as the team would have to lunge against the traces to back the heavy wagon up the hill.

Mace looked around for a fallen tree or sturdy branch he might use as a lever to lift the wagon. Seeing none, he walked around the wagon, set the brake tightly against the wheel, and returned to the girl.

'It's a bit of a problem, isn't it?' the girl said, obviously having considered all options before deciding to remove her dress.

Mace flashed her an easy smile. 'For a damsel in distress, a gentleman must rise to the occasion.'

She laughed. 'Yes, like simply lifting the corner of the wagon high enough to raise the wheel an inch or two off of the ground. Ought to be a snap. I doubt it would mean lifting more than two or three hundred pounds.'

'Precisely,' he said.

The girl's eyes widened with incredulity as Mace put his back to the wagon and secured a solid handhold.

'You can't be serious!' she exclaimed. 'The wagon is much too heavy to – '

By keeping his back straight and using the strength of his legs, he leaned back against the wagon bed. With a mighty heave, using every ounce of his strength, Mace raised the corner of the wagon. The vehicle groaned and hesitated – then the wheel came off the ground barely high enough for her to yank the dress free. He didn't hold the position a split-second longer than necessary, lowering it at once, exhausted from the extreme effort.

'Good heavens!' the girl exclaimed. 'I'd have sworn only Bruno was strong enough to lift our wagon by himself.'

'It was only one corner of the wagon,' he reminded her, still winded. 'I do that whenever I come upon a young lady with her dress pinned beneath the wheel.'

She smiled at his remark and began to brush the dirt from her dress. It had been a calico, but it was a dusty gray from the powdery sand at the bottom of the wash. As she dusted herself off, Mace was struck by the wholesome beauty of the girl. Not ravishing – the sort to take away a man's breath – she was endowed with a more subtle comeliness, like a girl Nature had smiled upon.

'I think it will come clean with a good washing,' he offered his opinion.

For the first time, the girl rewarded him with a genuine smile. It was thin-lipped and hesitant, but it was a smile.

'I've looked worse, I suppose. It's just that – well, I hate to go into town looking like I've been run over by a herd of horses.'

'Why did you stop, if you don't mind my asking?'

She visibly gulped her embarrassment. 'I saw those wild flowers – '

she pointed at some delicate blue blossoms – 'and I thought they would look nice on the dinner table.' She laughed softly at the absurd situation. 'Pretty dumb reason for getting myself in such a predicament, huh?'

'Not if you like flowers,' he defended her impulse. 'I've always found they make a house more homey.'

Her gaze was expressive. 'How refreshing to hear a man make such a statement.'

'I prize myself on having an eye for beauty.' He allowed his glance to appraise her shortly. 'And I know beauty when I see it.'

A slight flush told him the girl had not missed his forthright flattery. She looked away at once, reaching around to the back of her dress, trying to redo the buttons. She fumbled a moment, then sighed.

'I hate to be a bother,' she said rather meekly, 'but my fingers are so dusty and dirty, I can't do-up the back of my dress.'

Mace was smart enough to refrain from making any witty off-hand remarks. Sometimes his wit was keen, sometimes it was only half on target, and occasionally, it got him punched or slapped. He chose to remain silent and moved over behind her.

She had undid the top three buttons, revealing a creamy white neck and upper back. He swallowed his admiration and began to hook the three buttons, trying not to pop a thread or tear any fabric. He picked up a scent of the girl's hair – recently washed using a sweet-smelling soap or shampoo. So engrossed was he in working at such an unfamiliar chore, he didn't hear the approach of another rider.

His senses returned as the newcomer had dismounted ... and unexpectedly charged at him like an enraged bull!

Mace ducked a wild swing, pushing the girl out of the attacker's path. She yelped a feminine 'Eek!' in surprise, as a second flying fist missed Mace's head by mere inches.

Glimpsing the face of the young man named Rodney, who had held Su Lee during the encounter with Bruno, Mace halted his retreat and met him head-on. Blocking a third punch, he drove his doubled fist into the young man's stomach. The well-placed rock-hard set of knuckles took all the wind from his lungs and the fight out of him, both at the same time.

'Rodney!' the girl screamed at him. 'Are you crazy! What do you think you're doing?'

He couldn't reply, due to coughing and choking, with both arms across his stomach. In fact, he could not even remain standing, flopping to a sitting down position on the dusty trail.

'How dare you sneak up on us and attack this man!' she scolded him. 'He was helping me out of a sincere dilemma!'

Rodney gasped, tears in his eyes from trying to suck wind back into his lungs. 'Looked ... ' he panted to gulp another breath of air. 'Looked like he was undoing your dress!' His chest heaved as he swallowed enough air to speak again. 'He's the sidewinder who hit Bruno when he wasn't looking yesterday. Didn't give him a chance to defend himself!'

The girl's eyes flashed to Mace, but there was no scorn or criticism in them, only curiosity.

'You're Mace Banyon?'

Mace doffed his hat. 'At your service, fair lady.'

She smiled. 'At least you have the courtesy to not call me *ma'am*.'

'I've found that age is a factor in using the term,' he explained. 'Plus, having met you, I know you to be a lady.'

'Actually, I'm Mercy Paxton,' she introduced herself. 'The overly protective and impetuous clown sitting on his duff is my brother, Rodney.' Casting a warning eye at him, she added: 'We are *both* pleased to meet you.'

He smiled. 'I'm glad to meet a couple of my neighbors, even under the rather bizarre circumstances.'

'You must stop by for tea or lemonade one of these days,' she offered.

xxx

'It would by my pleasure, Miss Paxton.' He told her, but put a firm warning in his expression, as he fixed his gaze on Rodney. 'As for you, young fella, I overlooked your part in the harassment of one of my employees yesterday. I won't be so forgiving if it happens again.'

Rodney glowered at Mace, but he held his silence. With what dignity he could muster, he stood up and brushed off the seat of his britches.

'I've been hit before, but it never knocked the slats out of me.'

Mace grinned. 'It's called the solar plexus – a doctor once told me. Takes the wind out of just about anyone.'

'Guess I ought to thank you for only hitting me once.'

Mace put his attention back on Mercy. 'I'll leave your brother to the chore of the last button on your dress. I only manged to get two of them before his interruption.'

'Thank you for your help, Mr Banyon,' Mercy said. 'And good luck to you with your new job.'

Mace climbed aboard his horse and headed on down the trail. He figured he was going to need some luck. Providing a helping hand seemed to have endeared him to Miss Paxton, but her brother was obviously on the other side. As these were his closest neighbors on this side of the valley, he would like to have them as friends ... especially Mercy Paxton!

***

Mercy watched the erect back of Mace Banyon. From his ease atop the horse, he had obviously spent much of his life in the saddle. She was impressed by his air of assurance, a flowing self-assurance that made him seem both approachable and trustworthy. Not the most handsome man she'd ever met, he was attractive in a rugged, no nonsense sort of way. An odd contraction considering he had cold-cocked Bruno with a pick handle. And, when taken by surprise, he had avoided Rodney's unwarranted attack and put him on the ground with a single punch. He was not the ordinary type of man she was used to.

With a sigh of regret over not having more time to get to know the man, she glared at her brother. 'That was one stupid stunt, Rodney. If you'd have come in with your gun in your hand, Mr Banyon might have killed you!'

'Well, what was I supposed to think, Mercy?' he whined. 'I ride up and see this jasper unbuttoning your dress, and – '

'He was doing me up – not undoing me!' she snapped, cutting him off at the knees.

'How could I tell the difference?" he lamented. 'I didn't know what was going on.'

'A rational human being would have stopped to ask,' she continued her tongue-lashing. 'I wasn't struggling or fighting against him was I? No!' She was still fuming. 'I was standing with my back to him and my hands together in front of me. Did that look like he was doing something against my will?'

'All right,' he said, adequately humbled by her verbal dressing down. 'So what was he doing here? I was trying to catch you before you got all the way to town. Pa broke his favorite shovel handle and wanted you to pick up another one.' Finally, he took a moment to look at her disheveled appearance.' Now tell me,' he said, 'how come your dress wasn't done up?'

She explained the incident to him and he shook his head.

'Great,' he muttered cynically. 'Every time a girl is in distress, he shows up ... a regular hero.'

'That's right!' she snapped. 'And what did he mean about your harassment of his help?'

Rodney's shoulders drooped with his shame. 'I told you about it last night. It's when Banyon attacked Bruno without warning.'

'You told me and father it was a fight between Bruno and Tincup, but why would Tincup take on a man half his age and twice his size?'

'It was all in fun,' Rodney tried to end the inquisition. 'I was having a few drink with Bruno and Renz.'

'First thing in the morning?'

He avoided her hard gaze. 'I spent the night at the saloon – all right? It was a card game for the most part, and then I had a few drinks afterward.'

'You're becoming a drunk, Rodney,' she declared. 'So tell me what started the fight in the first place.'

'When Bruno saw the Chinese girl – Su Lee -- walk past, he said we should have a little fun with her. We weren't intending her any harm, just a little teasing.'

'Big tough, honorable men you choose to drink with, Rodney. Three of you picking on one Chinese girl. How very brave you are.'

'Cut it out, sis!' he yelped. 'I was drunk at the time.'

'And who can you blame that on?'

'Renz bought most of the drinks, so it's not like I was spending a lot of money.'

'It could have cost you your life!'

He wrinkled his brown. 'What do you mean?'

'*Mace Banyon* is what I mean. Father told me he carried a badge for several years and has killed a number of outlaws.'

'Being slick with a gun don't mean anything. If he hadn't hit me in the stomach …. '

He'd have knocked the head off of your shoulders!' she finished the sentence.

'Oh, yeah?'

'He picked the wagon up high enough that the wheel came off the ground, Rodney.' She pointed at the deep rut. 'I was lying in that hole and had no way to escape. He couldn't use the team to move the wagon, so he lifted it up with his bare hands.'

Rodney looked at the wagon, then back at his sister. 'You're joshing me. I'm not sure Bruno could have lifted that corner high enough to get the wheel off of the ground.'

Mercy shook her head. 'I'm dead serious. He put his back to the wagon and lifted it by himself. I shudder to think what he could have done to you.'

Rodney swallowed a dry lump in his throat, then said meekly: 'How about I do up that last button for you, sis. And I promise not to start another fight with Mace Banyon.'

'Yes, I think you ought to give him a wide berth from now on.'

'Wide berth, my foot! I'll cross the street if I see him coming.'

Mercy laughed. 'At last, my brother has seen the light.'

He chuckled. 'And the next time I see some strange man helping you in or out of your dress, I'll have the good sense to ride on by without casting a second glance.'

'I don't expect that to happen again,' she said. 'One time is embarrassing enough.'

Rodney hooked the last button and gave her a hand up onto the wagon.

'Seeing as how we're this close to town, I'll ride in with you.'

'Just so you don't think it gives you a reason to go into one of the saloons. I don't want you drinking any more.'

'OK, sis.' He grinned, 'So long as you don't want me drinking any less!'

They laughed together and started toward Oasis.

Chapter Four

Mace rode into the yard and spotted Tincup sitting in a rocking chair on the porch. The old gent shouted an order and Tong Lee hurried out of nowhere to take his horse.

Tincup displayed a grin as Mace stepped up on the porch.

'You can bet your mount will be curried, brushed, and ready for you at a moment's notice. In fact, if the horse is tired, you'll have a new mount waiting. You couldn't hire anyone else who is as quick to please as your two main house employees.'

'How did they happen to get stuck with duties here at the main house instead of getting a farm of their own?'

Tincup laughed, pointed to and waited until Mace took a seat, then replied. 'Old Tong Lee and me been together since before his wife died. Su Lee was only ten or eleven at the time. Little girl that she was, she took on the household chores and did most of the cooking. She got educated nights and was soon teaching any of the others who wanted to learn to speak English. Tong Lee never cared for farming, but he loves horses. With his daughter willing to tend to the house chores, it works out for everyone.'

'And where does Tong sleep at nights?'

'There's a room in the barn, so he can keep an eye on the animals after dark. He's a light sleeper so he will hear you if you get up in the wee hours of the morning to go somewhere.'

Mace leaned back on the chair and put his feet up on the porch railing. 'Ah-h,' he sighed. 'This is the kind of job I thought I had signed up for.'

'Yep, I keep a check on the farms – usually every day or two –so we can deal with any problems. At the end of the month, it will be up to you to run any figures for expenses and add in any income from the farms. Temple likes an itemized accounting at the end of every month, along with a progress report. Doesn't amount to much.'

'What about the bills, the mortgage and such?'

'Temple has to use Havelock's bank, but he does everything with transfers, so there is a record of every penny. Havelock charges a fee, but he has to keep it within reason or Temple will start issuing checks through Wells, Fargo. They have an office over in Springdale – about fifty miles from here.'

'How about credit?'

'The Chinese keep their own accounts in town with the general store in the Chinese district. Chen, who runs the store, gets whatever they need and charges fair prices.'

Are these sharecroppers making enough money to get ahead?'

'Most are doing OK. I figure they would be considered downright rich in their homeland. Many of them support families back there out of their earnings, so it will take them longer to get much equity in their farms.'

'So things are going pretty good, I mean, other than the banker trying to run our people out of the country so he can swoop in and take the land.'

Tincup removed his hat and scratched his balding scalp. 'Well, there is one little social-type problem.'

'And what's that?'

'It's kind of hard to explain ... to a newcomer like yourself. It's about Su Lee.'

'What about her?'

'She'll be getting married soon.'

'No more house-girl, huh?' Mace asked.

Tincup continued to frown. 'Nope, but that ain't exactly the problem.'

'Then what *is* the problem, Kelly? Am I supposed to guess?'

'Tong wants her to marry Ti Fat, but she favors Liu Yung,' Tincup finally blurted out. 'It's getting real complicated.'

'What's complicated about it?' Mace wondered. 'Su Lee is an American. She can marry whomever she wants to.'

'There's heritage and tradition at stake, Banyon. She only has the right to make her wishes known.'

'You mean Tong will decide.'

'It's not much different for many of the women in our culture – fathers are supposed to know and do what is best for their daughters.'

Mace didn't know why this was his problem, but he stuck to the subject. 'Tell me about the two suitors. Why does Tong want Ti Fat?'

'Because he thinks the man would be a better provider. The Chinese way is that when a girl marries, her husband's family is her own, and there is no going back to her old family. Ti has two brothers and a strong family, while Liu Yung is here alone. He only has one distant relative who works in town. He doesn't have as much to offer.'

'And what's your take on the two men.'

'I'd take Liu in a minute. He's a hard worker, smart, and he speaks better English than Ti Fat. He is also closer to Su Lee's age and is the better looker of the two.'

'What can I do about the problem, Kelly?'

'We've got twelve families, not counting Liu. The farms are divided up into sixteen parcels of land, so some are larger than others, with the bigger families having been given the larger acreages.'

'I'm still listening. What do you want me to do?'

'If you were to give Liu the place across from the Paxtons – there is already an empty house on the land – it would elevate him to a higher position than Ti Fat. He must still share his land with his brothers.'

Mace stared at Tincup. 'I didn't know Cupid chewed tobacco and wore cowboy boots.'

'Aw, it ain't that, Mace. It's just that Su Lee is as close as I'll ever have to a child of my own. I watched her grow up and she calls me her uncle.'

'Yeah, and I'll bet it's whenever she wants something.'

'You've been around her enough to know she's about the sweetest girl in the country. I can't tell you how much I worry about her happiness. You have to -- '

Mace raised a hand. 'Whatever you want is fine with me, Tincup. You go ahead and give Liu the house and assign him the land. However, I don't want any feuds between the different families over this.'

'No problem. Ti Fat's father is the one pushing him at Su Lee. He knows she is already in love with Liu. There are so few girls around that the fathers start trying to grab each one as she comes of age for one of his sons.'

'You've got my blessing, Cupid. Do whatever is necessary.'

Tincup should have been smiling, but he wasn't. 'Uh, there's just one other thing.'

'Now what?'

'I can't talk to the old man, 'cause he knows that I'm siding with Su Lee. Maybe you could have a word with him, tell him Liu is getting his own place ... you know, to smooth things over.'

Mace let out a slow breath. 'Let's get it over with then. I'm not much on playing the matchmaker.'

'You'll do just fine,' Tincup chirped, jumping to his feet. He patted

Mace on the shoulder as he hopped off the porch and headed for the barn.

Trying to sort out what he was going to say to the old man, Mace wondered how he'd got roped into a personal matter his first full day on the job. Maybe Tong wouldn't want a nosy boss butting into his affairs. He would probably listen out of respect, then do whatever he had planned anyway.

Tong appeared almost immediately and approached to the porch step. He waited until Mace pointed at the chair Tincup had vacated. He seemed very uneasy, sitting down across from his new supervisor.

'Tong Hing Lee, other than last night, I haven't had much time to talk to you.'

'Very sorry, Mr Banyon. I wish please you alla' time.'

'No, it's not your work,' Mace assured him. 'Tincup says you do a fine job and I certainly have no complaints. I've added another two dollars a month to your pay, as I promised.'

'Very good of you, Mr Banyon. I thank you very much.'

'Your daughter is an excellent worker too – good cook, keeps a clean house – I've no complaints about her either.'

'Very good daughter,' he agreed with a smile.

'I'm told she will marry soon.'

He bobbed his head. 'Time for her to raise own children, be wife and mother.'

Banyon smiled. 'I think she'll make a very fine wife and mother.'

Tong smiled again, still waiting for what Mace wanted to say.

'I'll need another housekeeper. Do you have anyone in mind for the job?'

Tong thought for a moment. 'No many girl working farms. Some children, but no girl old enough. Maybe use houseboy. Liu Yung has no farm. He help in town.'

'I've already found a place for him,' Mace replied to the suggestion. 'He's going to farm the forty acres up next to the Paxton place. I'm giving him the house and setting him up to sharecrop like the others. I imagine he'll need some help, as the land over there hasn't been under the plow yet.'

The old man was no fool. 'Why Liu Yung? We have many who would do well for you.'

'He's smart, speaks fair English, and I'm told he would like to start his own family. With him not having any close relatives, he needs a wife and some kids more than most of the others. They all have bigger families, while he has only is a distant cousin.'

'But he has no brother, no family. If Liu Yung die, he no have brother to marry wife.'

'At one time,' Mace said, trying to sound philosophical, 'there was only one Lee in all of China. What if that man hadn't taken a wife for himself? There would have been no more Lees. Yung needs to start a family of Yungs or his name will die with him.'

Tong considered his words ... and his proposal. 'You have some wisdom,' he said. 'Why do you not have wife? There many women in this country – only few Chinese girls.'

'If I do well in this job, I'll be able to start courting a young lady or two. That's one reason I need a reliable man for the empty plot of land.'

'What you say ... it is for my daughter's choice for husband?'

'Like you, Tong, I'd like to see her happy and married to a man she loves. I thought this might even up the scales – give you a chance to make the same choice as her.'

'I will try and find you housekeeper,' Tong said at last. 'Will that be all?'

'Yes,' Mace replied. 'Thanks for this little talk.'

With another bob of his head, Tong left the porch. A sly smile was on his lips, as if he was thinking of something pleasant. Mace assumed it would be pleasant for Su Lee as well.

***

A couple of hours after dinner, which he shared with Tincup, and the old boy headed off to his own home. Mace retired for the evening too. He had just hung his gun on the bedpost and put his hat on a night table, when a knock came at his bedroom door. He bid them enter and was surprised to see a very different-looking Su Lee. Her long hair was not braided as usual, but brushed out to delicately decorate her face, making her much more attractive.

'Su Lee?' he queried her visit.

She said not a word, but crossed to where he was standing ... then flung her arms around his neck and hugged him tightly. She held him that way for several seconds, then pushed back. Tears glistened in her dark eyes.

'What' is it? He asked worried something tragic had happened. 'What's the matter?'

She gave her head a negative shake. 'Nothing is wrong,' she said softly. 'Everything is wonderful. I can never thank you enough, Mr Banyon.'

'Thank me for what?'

'My father has agreed to allow me to marry Liu Yung, the man I love. Tincup told me about you giving him a house of his own, on the vacant land up by the Paxton boundary.'

Mace cleared his throat, uncertain as how to appropriately accept her thanks. 'Well, your father wanted you to be happy; he also wanted the best man for your future. I didn't do anything, except to follow Tincup's suggestion about those few acres of land.'

'We won't let you down, Mr Banyon,' she promised. 'Liu Yung and I will make you proud of your choice.'

He smiled down at her, feeling a warmth surge through his being at seeing such happiness. 'I'm glad things worked out for you. You deserve to wed the man you choose. Do you have a date for the wedding yet?'

'Pretty soon. Maybe in a week or two. First I must clean the house, buy the things we'll need – a nice bed, pots and pans, a table and chairs – the place has only a fireplace, so that is something we may have to deal with.'

'As a wedding present, I will – that is, the Temple Development company and I – we will give you a present of one hundred dollars. That should pay for most everything you need to set up housekeeping.'

'Really?' she was aghast. 'But you have only been here a couple days. You hardly know anything about me, about Liu Yung!'

'We aim to keep our tenant farmers happy,' he said. 'Less chance of them moving out in the middle of the night and leaving us high and dry.'

She laughed, not because he had said something funny, but because of her elated emotions.

'Should I be seeing you like this?' Mace asked in a whisper. 'I mean, with your hair down like it is?'

'The Manchus force the Chinese to wear their hair in braids. Without that symbol of loyalty, we cannot return to our homeland. As I told you before, I'm an American ... this is my homeland. I braid my hair out of respect for my father.'

He uttered a 'Whew! For a minute there, I was afraid if your father walked in on us, I might have to marry you myself. I thought the braids had some religious significance or something.'

'Many Chinese who come to this country do it only to earn enough money to live a decent life back home. Some of the tenant farmers have wives and children back in Canton and are supporting them. One day, when they have enough money, they will return home.'

'For you, being born in this country, I guess you can't miss something you never had.'

'I do miss some of the things my father speaks of. China has a far more orderly society than we do here, and most have a deep respect for other people. There are a few gangs and warlords who promote violence, but it isn't the norm.'

'While we have guys like Bruno and Renz, who pick on your people because they are Chinese.'

'Yes. I know the true reason is Mr Havelock's desire to own all of the rich land here along the river. Our crops far surpass what the dry farmers can raise.'

Deciding to end their conversation, he took her hand between his own and displayed a solemn expression. 'In case we don't get a private moment like this again, Su Lee, I wish you the very best. I hope you and Liu Yung will be very happy together.'

She smiled in return. 'Thank you, Mr Banyon. Thank you for everything.'

He said goodnight and she bowed her head slightly and backed through the door. As it closed, he stood for a long moment. Su Lee remained vivid in his mind's eye, haunting him. He had come to manage an estate for the money offered. But now, now he knew he would do whatever it took to keep these farmers safe – his farmers.

Temple had known what he was doing, hiring Mace. He knew of the jealousy and envy against his farmers, due to them working prize parcels of land. Even a poor farmer could make a good living when the ground was fertile and water was readily available all summer long. Havelock wanted the land for himself and had hired men to harass and try to drive out the Chinese.

Mess with my farmers ... you mess with me,' Mace vowed to himself. *Mess with me ... and I'll darn well mess up your life!*

Chapter Five

Several uneventful days passed, and Banyon was in the business section of town, shopping. He was picking out a new pair of socks when he felt someone's eyes on him. He turned slightly to meet the candid gaze of Mercy Paxton. She rewarded his alertness with a fleeting smile.

'I wondered if you were going to notice me,' she teased. 'I never knew selecting the perfect pair of socks was so enthralling.'

'I didn't recognize you, not being pinned under a wagon,' he teased.

'Not a very ladylike position to be caught in,' she admitted. Then with a girlish laugh. 'I'm just glad you didn't show up a minute or so later.'

He tried mightily not to let his imagination run away with that statement. 'I'm glad it was only a silly accident and not tragic. I'd have been very little help if the wagon had rolled over your legs.'

She grew serious. 'I spoke to my brother, and he wants you to know he is sorry for the way he acted – both at the wagon and in town.'

'I made allowance for his protective brotherly defense, and he had been drinking when he was with Bruno and Renz. I don't condone that kind of behavior -- whether drunk or sober -- but I'm willing to overlook it this one time. Is he with you here today?'

'No, he's working the upper field of hay. It's time for our first cutting. We ran out of twine, so I came into town to pick some up.'

'Twine?'

'We have one of those new balers that roll the hay. You use the twine to tie them off in bundles or bales. Then we can haul them to some or the ranchers up north – they actually get snow there and need winter feed for their livestock.'

'I'm familiar with stacking hay for the winter. I'm surprised it pays well enough to raise it as a crop here in farm country.'

'We rotate the crops and alfalfa grows long enough each season to get three and sometimes four cuttings. It makes it profitable.'

'I've heard of those balers, but I've never seen one. I'll have to ride out that way and see one at work.'

She smiled, flashing bright white teeth. 'You're welcome anytime.'

He bid her goodbye and paid for the things he had picked up. Casting a last glance at Mercy, Mace started out of the store. He didn't make it to the door, for young Mrs Havelock blocked his path. She had a worried look on her face.

'Don't go that way, Mr Banyon.'

'What? Why?'

'My husband is up the walk. Bruno is waiting for you. If you go out there, that vicious brute will beat you to death!'

He studied her upturned face and knew the lady was telling the truth.

'If I go out the back way, your husband might think you warned me.'

A flash of fear paled her complexion, but her eyes did not waver. 'I'll take that chance.'

He shook his head. 'I won't. You didn't come right out and say so, but I know Havelock's type. They bully anyone and everyone, either by their size or by the power of their money.'

'But Bruno will try and kill you with his bare hands – he can do it too!'

'I appreciate the warning, Mrs Havelock, but I'm not a man who runs from trouble.'

She expelled an exasperated sigh. 'I knew you would not listen to reason.'

'Thank you again for the warning, Mrs Havelock,' he said. Summoning his courage, he went out into the sunlight.

Bruno stood in the street alone, but was already surrounded by fifteen or twenty spectators. Everyone was ready to watch the new man get beaten into the dust, while the sheriff was not to be seen.

Havelock was leaning against the door of his bank – obviously closed until after the forthcoming fight. A satisfied smirk was pasted on his thick lips.

'I bet Renz ten bucks you wouldn't have the guts to face me fair and square,' Bruno challenged.

Mace glanced around and saw the gunman a short way off. His hand rested on the butt of his gun. If Mace decided on gunplay, he would be lucky to get off a shot. Rather than reply, Mace reached into his sack and removed the new pair of deer-hide gloves he had just paid for. Shame to get them bloody the first time he wore them, but he wanted to protect his hands.

'So, Bruno,' Mace said easily, 'I talked to a man who knew your mother. He said she tried for three days to get you to stay under the rock she found you under.'

'Funny,' he snarled.

'Said you were so repulsive,' Mace continued, 'your poor mother couldn't stand to have you near her. If not for the sow having a small liter, you would have starved for your daily milk.'

'You got a smart mouth, Banyon,' Bruno growled, his face dark with rage. 'I think I'll close it for you.'

'I'm sure you won't let ordinary reason or the fear of death stop you,' Mace replied, faking a bravado he didn't feel.

Moving toward Mace, Bruno vowed: 'I'm gonna rip your head off and let the kids kick it around like a tin can.'

Mace set his package on the porch of the general store and slipped on his gloves. He started forward to meet the big brute. 'No fair breathing in my face,' he taunted. 'Or lifting your arms up so I get knocked down by your body odor.'

'You're a real joker, you are!' Bruno snarled, his face black with pent-up rage. 'Let's see how funny you feel when I break all of your bones!'

Mace took up a fighting stance, his every sense peaked. He would need all of his skill and strength against Bruno ... and it might not be enough.

Bruno lunged forward swinging a vicious fist that would have knocked Mace into next week, had he not jumped to one side. He ducked a second roundhouse blow, but Bruno did not let up. He followed Mace in a circle, throwing punches that would have battered him to a pulp if they had connected.

Mace began to jab and poke, but kept out of the man's reach. He stung Bruno with a shot to the bridge of his nose – the still discolored portion where he had hit him with the pick handle. It only enraged the man even more.

Mace kept dodging and dancing, moving away from most of Bruno's deadly attack. However, the man was strong and his counter punches did little to slow him down.

Then something crashed against Mace's head and the taste of blood and dirt filled his mouth. He looked up, surprised to find himself on the ground. Bruno was grinning, even as blood seeped from his nose.

Slowly, gulping in what air he could, Mace got back to his feet. He ducked Bruno's next blow and reversed his tactics, lowering his head and driving it hard and upward under the big man's chin. It staggered him back a step, while Mace drove both fists at his mid-section, trying to find a way to do enough damage to bring the bully down.

But Bruno was game, and he was proud, battling back – both men giving and taking punishment. The fight dragged on until the pair were like two waltzing rag dolls, moving in slow motion. Both men were in a kind of trance, each wondering what was holding the other one up. In a total blitz, both men unleashed blows at the same time, hitting one another with every last ounce of strength they had. Mace caught the bigger man, with the hardest shot he could manage, squarely on the jaw. In the same instant, a massive fist connected to the side of his own head --

For the second time, Mace found himself on the ground. He rolled away, thinking Bruno might kick him while he was down, but it didn't come. Rising to his knees, Mace stared in awe at Bruno, who was also on the ground, face-down a few feet away.

'It's over!' a feminine voice declared. 'The fight is over!'

'Yeah?' Mace asked densely, unable to get his feet under him. 'Who won?'

'Hurry! Before Bruno gets up again!' It was Mercy Paxton's voice in his ears. Then her hands took hold of his arm and she helped him to stand. 'Come on,' she coaxed. 'I'll get you home.'

***

There was a coolness about Mace's brow, easing the throb in his head. His face and ribs felt as if they'd been ground to powder, and each breath brought fire to his lungs. He couldn't open one eye and was certain his body must be broken in ten places.

'Just try and relax, Mr Banyon,' Su's voice soothed. 'I will make you something to drink that will make you feel better.'

He opened his mouth, but no words were at hand. Every fiber, every bit of skin and muscle, felt bruised and swollen.

'Will he be all right?' a second feminine voice asked. It sounded like Mercy.

'You need not worry about Mr Banyon,' Su informed her. 'I will tend to him. He will be fine.'

'But shouldn't' we have the doctor come see him?'

'He has no broken bones, no cuts to treat. The doctor would waste his time.'

'Yes, but – '

'I will take good care of him, Miss Paxton. You may stop by in a few hours if you wish. He needs to rest.'

Banyon thought Su Lee was right. He ceased trying to stay awake and fell into a deep slumber.

For the next few hours, he remained in a state of pain-free limbo, never quite able to sort out the real world from the fantasy world of broken dreams. He ate or drank several times, but wasn't sure if he had actually done it or imagined it. When he finally fought to full consciousness, he opened his good eye to discover the room was dark.

'Are you awake?' Su Lee asked.

He turned his head a little, able to see her next to the bed. Her hair was loose about her shoulders, and she had been running a comb through the gossamer-like strands. She wore a robe and slippers.

'Did I sleep all day?'

She smiled. 'All day, all night, and all day. I think you must have exhausted every ounce of strength in your body fighting against Bruno.'

'I couldn't take on a rowdy four-year-old and win at the moment.'

'You gave a fine show of strength, leaving the street under your own power with only Miss Paxton's help. It took three men to carry Bruno off of the street.' She paused. 'Miss Paxton seemed quite concerned about your welfare. She came by yesterday, but you were asleep. I think she likes you.'

'She's indebted to me,' he dismissed her observation. 'I helped her out of a fix a while back.'

'I am not blind to the feelings of another woman, ' she argued. 'The young lady will not tell you of her attraction, but it is there to see.'

Mace asked, 'What makes you so smart, Su Lee?'

She laughed. 'You can see into the hearts of other men, but only a woman can see into the heart of another woman.'

'I'm impressed,' he told her. 'I didn't think even women could understand the nature of other females.'

'You are correct, Mr Banyon. We women are the more passive outwardly, but more complex inwardly.'

'Liu Yung is getting a real prize for a wife,' he said. 'I hope he knows how special you are.'

'If not, I will soon teach him,' she replied with a trace of humor.

'You should get some sleep, Su Lee. I'll be up and about in the morning.'

'Do you think there will be more trouble?'

Mace tried to muster a smile of confidence, but the effort hurt his swollen face. "Nothing I can't handle. You just worry about what you're going to feed me for breakfast.'

'That is no problem,' Su said, again with a trace of humor. 'You will have a nice bowl of mush.'

'Wonderful,' he said laconically. 'It will take me a month to heal.'

'Mush will suffice until you can chew solid food again. Besides,' she added with a lilt to her voice, 'it will encourage you to recover that much quicker.'

'Good night, Su Lee,' he grunted through his puffy lips.

'Yes, good night to you, Mr Banyon.'

Staring at the dark ceiling, Mace wondered what kind of stunt Havelock would try next. The man ran a bank and had a sizable mansion to manage. However, his place was on the poor side of the valley, which made him appear outwardly to favor the dry farmers. He also had hired men – Whitey, Renz and Bruno – meaning his payroll was likely more than his earnings. If he was hurting for money, he wouldn't be offering to buy the Temple holdings unless they were near giveaway prices. The first order of business would be to run the tenant farmers off of their land.

Mace flexed the fingers of his right hand. The gloves had protected his knuckles. There was a little stiffness, but no broken or cracked bones in his hands. He knew the next battle would not be with fists, but guns. Having put his life on the line a number of times as a deputy marshal, he had done a great deal of practicing. Soon as he was able, he would brush up on his draw.

Even as he contemplated what action he should take to counter any move by Havelock, he allowed Su Lee's words to enter his head. Mercy liked him. She had seen the girl's concern and drew her conclusions. And, while he didn't know Su Lee all that well, she seemed an intelligent young lady. If she saw the attraction, it was there.

With the sentiment fresh in his mind, he fell asleep, with visions of Mercy Paxton dancing around in his brain.

Chapter Six

The next few days passed without incident. Mace was up and about, a purplish swelling around his eye evidence of his battle with Bruno. His ribs were sore and his muscles were stiff, but he was in good enough shape to make the rounds of his farms again.

The sun was growing hotter with each passing day, and there had been no rain in weeks. Many of the outlying farms were showing wilted or drooping crops, and their owners were worried. As for Temple's holdings, the irrigation water flowed daily, reaching the parched fields often enough to perk up and invigorate the plants.

Sitting at the edge of the Paxton farm, Mace looked at the clear, cloudless sky. A drought would increase the resentment toward the bottomland workers. Watching their own fields wither and die, the other farmers would begrudge how the Temple farms were flourishing. It would be a weapon Havelock would certainly use.

Just then, Mace spotted the sheriff coming down the road, evidently going to see the Paxtons. Seeing Mace, Wilcox angled his horse over to him. There was no smile of greeting, no warmth in the sheriff's haggard expression. He looked like a worried man.

'Howdy, Sheriff,' Mace greeted him with a smile.

Wilcox simply nodded, stopping his horse next to Mace's sorrel. He appraised Mace with a critical eye before speaking.

'You don't look too bad, considering the man you tangled with. I'm surprised Bruno didn't break every bone in your body.'

'I'm sure he harbored the idea when he started the fight.'

'You know about the other trouble?'

Mace sat up straight. 'What trouble?'

'I've gotten three complaints from the nearby farmers about the Chinese.'

'What kind of complaints?'

Wilcox took a deep breath, as if sorting out his thoughts in a particular order. 'Barnes claims he saw a Chinese man cutting one of his fences. Hines reported the theft of several chickens. And one of Miller's calves disappeared. He figures it ended up smothered in rice and served on a plate.'

'So that's Havelock's game, is it?'

Wilcox's face darkened. 'Those Chinese farmers of yours could be stealing or doing some damage. There isn't any proof to the contrary, Banyon.'

'You strike me as an honest and moderately intelligent man, Sheriff,' Mace made the statement. 'These people have a high degree of honor. They are making a good living and would never stoop to stealing or destroying other people's property.'

Wilcox continued his hard gaze. 'It makes no difference what I believe, Banyon. If it comes to taking one person's word over another, I have to go with victims.'

'Is there any proof?' Mace asked. 'Has anyone actually recognized one of my people during the commitment of a crime?'

'If I had proof, I'd be riding out to arrest someone.'

'OK, Sheriff. We both know Havelock's end game. He wants all of the Temple land for his own. If Havelock is working this kind of angle, he is trying to reach a point where he can get a mob to run the Chinese out of the valley.'

'Don't you think I know that?'

'What I know, is that because we're in a drought, a lot of farmers are watching their crops die, while the places I oversee have access to the stream are able to irrigate and save their fields. As sheriff, you have to be the strongest voice of reason. You have to keep a lid on any gatherings. If Havelock gets a mob riled, there will be blood spilled. That's not something you or I want.'

'I work for those who pay my monthly salary, Banyon. That means I owe as much to Havelock and the other farmers as I do to the Temple holdings. I have to be on both sides.'

'No,' Mace corrected him, 'you have to be on the *right* side!'

Wilcox sighed. 'Right or wrong, far as I can tell, you have only one ally. Rodney Paxton stood up for a couple of Chinese yesterday. He put a stop to some hazing by a couple of people working the dry farms.' He shrugged. 'Kind of surprised me --- hell, it surprised everyone. But even with the Paxtons siding you, they don't carry much weight. After all, a good portion of their holdings is bottomland too, so the other farmers are jealous of them to start with.'

'I hadn't heard about Rodney's action,' Mace admitted. 'The Chinese never bring their complaints to me. If they are roughed up, cheated, or whatever, they seem to simply accept it and move on.' Instilling an icy frost to his voice, he added: 'I assure you, Sheriff, I am not so forgiving. If you wonder about my determination, ask Bruno if he thinks I mean what I say.'

He grunted. 'I don't doubt your sincerity, Banyon, but I have to follow the law. If someone points a finger at one of the Chinese, I'll arrest him. Judge Morrison is a fair-minded man. He was a lawyer as a younger man and worked for the railroad. He's familiar with immigrants of all kinds and will see through a frame-up. I have to do my job and I expect your cooperation in every way.'

Mace met the man with a level gaze. Wilcox had a point, but he wouldn't be much help in a fight. He was a peace-keeper, more than a peace officer. The fact he was fair in his judgment was his biggest asset.

'I'll do whatever I can to uphold the law – not Havelock's law, but the actual laws of our land. If things can be settled fairly, that's fine. But if push comes to shove, I'll use whatever force is necessary to protect

Temple's property and our workers.'

'I wouldn't expect any less,' Wilcox said.

There didn't seem to be anything left to say, so the sheriff raised a hand in farewell, riding on towards the Paxton farm. Mace wondered if he was going to warn old man Paxton to keep his son out of town, or tell them to mind their own business. Wilcox had an unenviable task, trying to keep peace in Oasis, with a full-scare war brewing.

***

A sudden outcry woke Mace from his sleep. He had his pants on when the door flew open to his room. Su Lee was out of breath, still in her nightdress.

'The Paxton farm is on fire!' she cried.

Tong had Mace's horse saddled and at the door by the time he reached the porch. Tincup – who had been staying at the house since Mace's fight with Bruno – rubbed the sleep from his eyes, coming out onto the porch.

'What's all the fuss?' he asked groggily.

'Get as many Chinese as you can over to Paxton's place – right now!' Mace shouted.

'Huh?' His eyes popped open wider. 'Do what?'

'Bring tools to fight a fire! Do it as quick as you can!' Mace called, swinging up onto the horse. He didn't look back as he bolted from the yard.

Racing down the dark road, Mace could see the red-orange glow dancing against the black curtain of the night. He guessed the direction as where their new crop of hay had been cut and stacked.

Mace arrived a few minutes later. Seeing the three Paxtons beating at the blames with blankets and shovels, he jumped off his horse and grabbed an extra spade. Working along side old man Paxton, they continued beating at the voracious conflagration.

'You and your damn Chinese!' the old man shouted. 'I saw one of them running away after setting fire to the field!'

'Where did he go?'

'Over the hill, at the head of the pasture. He had a horse waiting for him.'

Mace continued to beat at the hungry flames, but his mind was working. Most of the Chinese farmers used oxen or mules. He hadn't seen a single one who owned a horse. And what possible motive could there be for setting a fire at their only ally's place.

'You saw him?' Mace asked, between swats with his shovel. 'How do you know he was Chinese?'

'Funny hat, sash, and robe – the works!' Ed said, panting between the words.

Mace let it drop, trying to help cut a swath to try and make a firebreak to halt the progress of the raging fire.

The four of them had little chance of stopping the spread, but a dozen or more Chinese arrived via a wagon driven by Tincup. They all had tools and began to widen the swath to prevent the fire from reaching the next field. A few more men arrived on foot, all having run a mile or two to get there, carrying hoes and shovels. Within a short while, the fire was beaten back and burned itself out to mere embers.

Ed Paxton stood in the acrid, lingering smoke, looking around at the numerous workers who were smothering or smashing the final sparks. Soon, there was nothing more than the dying smoke hanging in the air.

'Let's go have a look up where you saw the man who set the fire,' Mace suggested. 'Might be a clue – some way for us to figure out who it was.'

Ed led the way to a small rise at the end of the hay field. As he reached the top, he pointed to the headgate on his irrigation ditch.

'He had his horse right there. I could see him moving about, but he had already set fire to the field. I hurried to get the kids out here to try and stop its spread.'

Mace looked at the ground carefully, then used a match to scrutinize a footprint. He stopped his search and motioned to Ed.

'Check out these prints,' he advised the senior Paxton.

Ed leaned over, looking closely at the ground. 'Boot prints,' he said. 'So what?'

Mace said, 'Tell me, when is the last time you saw a Chinese – any Chinese – wearing Western-style riding boots.'

Ed knelt down, fingered the groves in the ground, and looked up at Mace. 'You're right. They all wear those flat-soled sandals.'

'It's just what I was telling Wilcox to be on the lookout for, Mr Paxton. Havelock is behind this, trying to turn you against my farmers. Rodney stuck his neck out for a couple of them in town, and now your place is set on fire. Rather than wait until you were in bed, the man setting the fire intended that you should see him ... dressed the same as a Chinese farmer!'

Ed rose up to stand next to Mace. 'I'll have a talk with Havelock, by thunder! If he thinks he can set fire to my fields, he' got another think coming. I'll break him in half with my bare hands!'

Mace cautioned, 'We have no proof against him, but the horse left tracks. Come morning, I'll follow them and see where they lead.'

'I've got to do something,' Ed complained. 'I can't let him get away with this.'

'So make the rounds to the other farmers, the ones on the opposite side of the valley. Make sure they know this act of arson wasn't done by the Chinese. Let them draw their own conclusions as to who would stand to gain by your turning against us.'

Ed sighed, his reluctance evident. 'All right, Banyon. I'll play the fiddle by your tune for a spell.' Then the anger caused his voice to raise an octave. 'But Havelock isn't going to push me around. I've been in this valley since it was settled. Rodney and Mercy were both born in my house, and my wife and their mother is buried beyond the garden. I've got my roots in deep, and I'll die before I give an inch!'

Mace didn't have any words to add, so he patted the man on the shoulder. The two of them walked together back to where Mace had left his horse. All of the Chinese had left for their homes. Only Tincup remained, and he was talking with Rodney. However, it was Mercy who came forward to meet them.

Her face was blackened from the soot, with her hair in disarray from the wind and her vigorous efforts of fighting the fire. She offered a weary smile – similar to the first one he'd seen on her face.

'Nothing like a little exercise in the middle of the night to break up a sound sleep.'

'I was in bed as well,' Mace replied. 'Su Lee woke me up when she saw the glow from the fire.'

'Did you and Father find anything?'

'About what I expected,' Mace replied. 'Someone dressed as a Chinese – likely the same one who has been vandalizing and stole some chickens and a calf. He set the fire and made sure to be seen leaving the scene.'

'It has to be Havelock's doing,' Mercy said. 'He's been after the bottomland since he arrived a couple years ago.'

'Trouble is, we have no proof,' Mace said.

She scowled. 'It isn't right! He sets fire to our field, destroys our crops, and we have no recourse!'

'Like I told your father, I'll track the horse, soon as it's light, but the chances of finding out who was on the horse is pretty thin. I'm betting Havelock will have an alibi in place for the man responsible.'

Mercy appraised him for a moment, her expression softening. 'Su Lee seems to have mended your wounds and battle scars. You don't look the worse for wear after such a row with Bruno.'

'I still carry a couple memories,' he said. 'I wouldn't care to tangle with him again.'

'I imagine he feels the same way. Rodney saw him in town today, and he still looks pretty battered. His broken nose blacked both of his eyes. Clearly, you won the fight.'

'In a fight like that, Miss Paxton, there are no winners, just survivors. I prefer pick handles to fists ... ' with a grin, 'so long as I'm the one with the advantage.'

She laughed. 'Yes, it does save wear and tear on the body.'

Mace took the reins of his horse. 'I'll give you a ride back to your house,' he said.

She didn't refuse, accepting his help to mount. He swung up behind her and started for the main house. Tincup and Rodney were following along behind Ed Paxton. All of the Chinese had begun the trek back to their homes, for not all would fit in the buckboard Tong was driving.

With his arms around Mercy, Mace kept control of the reins and she sagged back against his chest. The battle against the fire had drained her strength. Mace has spent most of his energy as well, but he still felt a stirring at having such an attractive girl in his arms. Even covered in dirt, sweat and ashes from the fire, she was inviting, desirable.

'What will you do now?' the girl asked without turning in the saddle.

I think I'll keep you in my arms forever, he wanted to say. Instead, he grunted.

'Darned if I know, Miss Paxton. I only spoke to Havelock one time and we exchanged threats. If we try and retaliate, it might start the very war we want to avoid.'

'He has aroused many of the people in the valley, portraying the Chinese as the enemy, rather than the drought. It is hard for the dry farmers to look upon the green fields of the farms on our side of the valley, while they are watching their own crops die.'

'Temple owns the land Havelock covets,' Mace stated the obvious. 'Driving out the Chinese would do nothing to help any of the dry farms. If Silas chose, he could hold on to the land and sell it to another buyer or bring in Irish, Dutch or English pilgrims to assume the farms.'

'What if Havelock simply occupied the land, once your farmers abandoned their places? Could he somehow assume ownership?'

'Temple didn't acquire the land under the Homestead Act. It isn't Government owned, it's privately owned and deeded to him. He purchased it from people who had lived up to the terms of settlement.'

'Do you think Havelock knows that?'

'Probably doesn't matter to him. If he can get it cheap, he can simply buy the land.'

When Mace stopped the horse in the yard, Mercy hesitated, as if none to anxious to get down. She finally turned sideways, looking at him, her face only inches from his own. He fought down the desire to try and kiss her, knowing it would be foolish and impulsive. Regrettably, the desire was naked to see, right on the surface.

The girl saw the yearning in his eyes and quickly lowered her eyes, hiding whatever her response might have been. When she spoke, her voice was a whisper, rather husky, as if her own emotions were crowding her vocal cords.

'Be careful, Mace,' she used his first name. 'Havelock might turn loose Renz and Whitey if he thinks you're blocking his ambition. Whitey has a price on his head in both Montana and Wyoming for murder. According to Rodney, Renz is even more deadly with a gun. Either one of them could try and kill you.'

'I've dealt with men like them before,' he assured her. 'I won't take any chances I don't have to.'

She lifted her eyes and forced a tight smile. 'I'd better say goodnight. Father often runs eligible young men off of our place. I wouldn't want him running you off too.'

He grinned. 'Some things are worth a little risk ... and you are sure enough one of those things.'

Mercy flashed a coy smile, then swung her right leg over the pommel of the saddle and slid to the ground. She landed lightly on her feet and looked up at him again.

'Don't be a stranger, Mace. Come and visit us sometime. We are having fried chicken Sunday, if you happen to stop by.'

'I appreciate the invite ... Mercy,' he boldly reciprocated, using his first name. 'If I'm not tied up, I'll make a point of being here.'

She stepped back from his horse and lifted a hand in farewell.

Mace moved forward in the saddle as Tincup came over to his horse. He used an empty stirrup and climbed up behind Mace. Then the two of them rode out of the yard.

'War is comin', Mace said to Tincup. 'I believe Havelock thinks if he drives our farmers out, he can make Temple a cheap offer and buy him out.'

'Yeah, and it might be easier to sell than lose the crops for a full season, then have to hire men enough to not only man the farms but do battle against Havelock's goons. What are we gonna do about it?'

Mace grunted. 'The short answer – we win the war.'

Chapter Seven

Rodney Paxton rode into town early the next morning. He had thought to catch Havelock at home, but the yard-handyman said both he and his wife had already gone to work at the bank. Rodney tied up his horse in front of the bank, scanned the street for any of Havelock's men, and, seeing none, entered the building.

Lori Havelock looked up from the teller window where she worked every day. Her face showed a mixture of fear and concern at seeing him.

'Rodney!' she exclaimed in a hushed voice. 'What are you doing here?'

He didn't feel like passing the time when he had come on a mission to confront Havelock, but Lori was not a girl he could ignore, one he'd admired ever since he met her. It tore his insides apart that she was married to a tyrant, a despot who not only didn't deserve her, but didn't appreciate her. He had danced with her one time when Havelock had gotten drunk and passed out at a local barn dance. He still remembered how light and wonderful Lori felt in his arms as they circled the floor to the music.

'Do you know what your husband did last night?' he asked the girl, speaking quietly. 'He had one of his men set fire to our hayfield!'

Her immediate shock revealed her innocence. 'Seth did that?'

'Sent a man dressed up to look Chinese, trying to turn us against Banyon and his farmers. But Banyon and his workers all raced over to help save the field. We did manage to salvage about half of it.'

'I know nothing about what Seth does,' she vowed. 'He spends time with his men, but I refuse to have anything to do with them. When they visit the house, I go to my room.'

'I came to collect what he owes us.'

Lori's face displayed instant panic. 'No! Rodney! Don't you go into his office like this. He'll sic one of his men on you! Whitey or Renz could force you into a fight. They might even kill you!'

Rodney shook his head, steadfast. 'I've made up my mind, Lori. Your husband has used his money and men to run roughshod over everyone in the valley. It's high time he learns there are some people he can't push around.'

'But Renz ... Whitey ... '

'They won't hurt me. I've gotten drunk with both of them a good many times, and without Havelock, they're through.'

Lori put her hand up to her mouth, her eyes even wider with a horrified realization. 'You are going to challenge Seth to a gunfight?'

Rodney patted the gun at his hip. 'If I can.'

'Foolish boy!' a cold voice said from the door of the bank.

Rodney turned to face Havelock, but Seth had a gun leveled at his chest. He'd be dead in a second if he touched his gun.

The banker put cruel eyes on Lori. 'You planning my death, you traitorous little witch?'

'No, Seth!' she cried. 'And I know Rodney didn't mean what he said. He wouldn't draw a gun against you.'

A wicked simper curled the man's lips. 'Is that true, *Rod'ney*?' he slurred out his name. 'Were you only trying to impress my beautiful, deceitful little wife?'

Rodney bridled. 'You had our field set afire, Havelock. I came to demand payment for what we lost.'

The man showed no emotion. 'I hear it's the Chinese who are doing all of the dastardly deeds in the valley. I don't think any court would find me liable for their actions.'

Rodney was a hothead, known for his quick temper, but he knew when death was staring him in the eye. He controlled the impulse to draw or try any kind of offensive action. He knew the banker would kill him without hesitation. Dejected over the turn of events, he walked around the man and headed out the door.

'There'll be another time, Havelock. One day soon, you'll have to fight like a man and do your own dirty work. When that day comes, I'll be there.'

'Don't come back looking for trouble, Paxton,' Seth warned. 'The Chinese are the ones responsible for all of the problems in the valley. You would do much better to take our side in the upcoming war.'

Rodney stopped at the porch at his offer. 'I'm not alone in this fight, Seth. Mace Banyon knows you are behind everything that's happened. You got the drop on me, but I doubt you'll have the same luck with him.'

The banker didn't like having the newcomer thrown up in his face. 'Banyon is only one man. He got lucky against Bruno, but he won't be so lucky if he tries to take on Whitey or Renz. If he becomes too much of a nuisance, he will end up buried in a shallow grave.'

Rodney surprised him then. He laughed, as if the idea was absurd. 'You keep telling yourself that, if it allows you to sleep at night, Seth. But your time is coming.'

Havelock clamped is teeth together as Rodney mounted his horse and headed out of town. Three steps took him over to the teller's cage. He bore into Lori with a hot, smoldering gaze. He hated the automatic defiance that appeared in her expression.

'You're siding with another man against me, aren't you, Lori?' he demanded.

'Rodney Paxton is a nice boy. I didn't want to see the two of you fight. I was trying to sooth his anger when you arrived.'

'Sure you were, you conniving little witch! You chase after every man who comes sniffing around.'

Lori squared her shoulders. 'I've been completely faithful to you, Seth. I'm a Christian woman. I would never break one of the Commandments!'

'No?' he cracked a sinister grin. 'Honor thy husband...' he sneered. 'But you warned Banyon when Bruno was outside the store waiting for him.'

'I didn't want to see the man killed; I gave him the chance to run. He didn't take it.'

'And now you and Rodney, all cozy together, whispering words of love?"

'I told you,' she retorted. 'He came in with blood in his eye. I didn't want him to kill you, any more than I wanted you to kill him.'

He put his hands on his hips and continued to burn her with his hot glare. However, she was not as docile as when he had married her. She glared right back.

'A good *Christian woman*,' he grunted.

'You should try being a Christian yourself sometime, Seth.'

He chuckled, the tension of the moment gone. 'Yes, dear,' he mocked her comment. '*The meek shall inherit the earth*.' Then with a firm stance, 'but I'm not waiting to inherit anything. I want it now!'

***

Mace carefully studied the bootprints. They were rather narrow for most men, and the culprit had sank into the ground less than Mace's own prints. The stride was a couple inches shorter than his own natural step too.

So, the guy was smaller man than Mace ... perhaps five-foot-five or six, a hundred and twenty or thirty pounds. Renz was bigger than that, and Bruno's elephant feet would dwarf the prints. There had been mention of a man he had yet to meet – Whitey Curn. He wondered about his size.

Next, he concentrated on the horse's tracks. He hoped for a nick or a missing shoe, something irregular that would set him apart from other steeds, but he found nothing uncommon. As he'd guess the previous night, the tracks led into town and were lost by the heavy traffic. Mace had learned nothing from following the horse.

Even as he was thinking of his next move, he spied Rodney Paxton, on his way out of town. The young man had a gun tied down on his hip. He wondered what he was doing here so early in the morning. There didn't seem to be any excitement on the street, so he guessed that nothing major had taken place.

Mace stopped his little sorrel, staring at the bank. A talk with Havelock was in order, but what would it get him? He had no proof for any accusations he might make. He could go to Wilcox, but the sheriff would be just as negative – no proof, no support.

He needed to figure out who was masquerading as a Chinaman and doing the dastardly deeds. If he could expose the ruse and present one of Havelock's men as the perpetrator, it might quell the turbulent feelings that were being fanned against the tenant farmers.

Deciding against a useless confrontation with either man, Mace returned to his house. Tong was there at once to take charge of his horse, but there was more on his mind than doing the chore.

'Why the long face, Tong?' Mace asked.

'There be trouble, Mr Banyon. I tell Mr Kelly.'

'Tincup?' Mace looked around. 'Where has he gone to?'

'Ti Fat was unhappy losing Su Lee. He say nothing – him know Su Lee favor Liu Yung. Now he gone.'

'Gone?'

'Brothers' say he drink much rice wine. Then leave house. No one see him no more.'

'When did this happen?'

'Last night. Before fire. Mr Kelly go search.'

Mace asked, 'Has Ti Fat ever done this before — disappearing for a period of time?'

'Never all night. He like gamble, but Chinese not welcome in saloon. All families been asked, but no one see him.'

Mace took back the reins of his horse and mounted once more. He spoke to Tong from the saddle. 'With the rumor going around that a Chinese has been doing some vandalizing, his life might be in danger. Where did Tincup go to search?'

'In hills.' He pointed to beyond the Paxton farm.

Mace whirled his horse around, but did not start him out of the yard. Instead, a familiar form appeared, riding directly at him. It was Sheriff Wilcox ... and he had a body draped over the saddle in front of him. Mace was back on the ground by the time the sheriff stopped his horse.

'Someone dragged him right up to my doorstep,' was the man's sedate greeting. 'There was a note stuffed in his mouth warning the Chinese to get out of the valley.'

'He's dead?' Mace asked, knowing the answer.

'I didn't see who dropped the body at my door, Banyon. I made a quick circle to look around, but no one saw anything.'

'A fire was set at Paxton's place last night too,' Mace informed him. 'It seems Havelock's turning up the heat to make the valley boil.'

'I hadn't heard about the fire.'

'I'd like to take a look at your yard, if you don't mind,' Mace told him. 'You might have missed something.'

'You've more experience than me, Banyon,' the lawman admitted. 'However, if we find out who did this, it'll be my job to handle it, not yours.'

Mace didn't make any promise, helping Tong to lower Ti Fat to the ground. Tong hurried to fetch a blanket to wrap the body in.

The sheriff remained silent while the old man returned with a suitable cover. Mace helped wrap the body and spoke to Tong.

'You get word to Ti Fat's family and see to the body. Whatever must be done for him, you have my permission. The company will pay for any expenses – coffin, flowers, whatever.'

'I will take care of him,' Tong promised.

Mace again got on his horse and he and the sheriff rode out of the yard. They continued for about a mile, until they reached the Wilcox place on the far side of town.

The lawman's farm was only a few acres, fenced with poles and wire, and a wide gate at the front. The house was modest, two or maybe three rooms.

'You say someone dragged Ti Fat's body right up to your door?'

'Yep. One of them must have gotten down to open the gate and the other dragged the body up to the house. When I opened the door, the gate was closed and Ti Fat was lying next to the porch.'

'You found footprints from both men?'

'Yep. The man who dragged him had to retrieve his rope. His prints are pretty hard to read, but this guy opened the gate. He left a couple readable prints.'

Mace climbed down, examined the ground near the gate, and stood up straight. The markings were familiar, smeared by horses and the sheriff himself, but still recognizable They were inordinately narrow bootprints.

'One of the two killers is the same one who set fire to the Paxton place last night. He dressed up as a Chinaman and let himself be seen. It took a good many of my farmers to put out the fire, but Ed Paxton and I are convinced the man who set the fire was not Chinese.'

'How can you be so sure?'

'We find the man who wears those narrow boots, we find the one who's been doing the marauding and trying to incite the population against the Chinese.'

'So what does that give us? How are we supposed to find someone dressing up and doing mischief? Do we have to compare the size every man's boots in the whole valley?'

'No need. We know who the man works for.'

'Ah, Banyon,' Wilcox groaned. 'Don't even say it.'

Mace grinned. 'Can you think of a better place to start?'

The man gave a sad shake of his head. 'I can darn well think of *safer* places to start!'

Chapter Eight

Mace and Wilcox's first stop was the livery stable. The hostler, a thin man called Rufe, was eager to help, but he had been gone during the night. With his breath strong enough to stand on, there was little doubt what he'd done the previous evening. It was interesting to note he'd been given money for a bottle by Bruno and Whitey.

Mace had alerady dismissed Bruno as an arson suspect due to his size. As for Whitey, they spotted him having breakfast at a cafe, even though it was almost noon.

Mace and the sheriff remained out of sight and allowed him to finish his meal. When Whitey finally came out, they fell in a short way behind him. He remained unaware of them, cutting across the street between a wagon and several riders. The soft dirt of the street gave the two men an opportunity to survey his fresh bootprints.

'There you are, Sheriff.' Mace pointed to the marks. 'Those boots of his are special made, more narrow than ordinary boots, and he's not more than five-and-a-half feet tall. In the dark, wearing Chinese clothes, he could easily pass for one of them.'

'So it would seem,' Wilcox agreed.

'I'll go with you, if you think there might be trouble.'

The sheriff shook his head. 'If you went along it would start a fight. If I need a deputy, I'll come and get you.'

'You're the law in Oasis – as long as everyone obeys the law.'

Wilcox bobbed his head. 'I'll take care of this.'

Mace watched the man cross the street behind Whitey. He didn't like to let the sheriff handle it alone, but it was his choice. If Whitey didn't come freely, then it would be up to Wilcox to allow him to help.

Deciding to stick close by, Mace went to the cafe and ordered a meal. Sitting by a window, he watched the street while he was eating. He was nearly finished when the sheriff appeared. Wilcox saw him in the window, but chose to walk down to the bank and went inside. As for Whitey, he was not in sight.

Mace was done with the meal, but ordered a second cup of coffee, waiting to see what Wilcox was up to. A few minutes passed before the sheriff came out of the bank. He saw Mace was still at the cafe and walked over to the eatery. He didn't look happy as he joined Mace at his table.

'Stay offa' my back, Banyon,' he growled, the ire causing him to clench his teeth.

''What happened?' Mace asked, careful to keep the question simple.

'What do you think?' he snapped. 'Whitey was playing cards in the back of the saloon last night – all night long.'

'Says who?'

'Renz, Bruno, Havelock and the barkeep – Axle. Can't arrest a man with that kind of alibi. The judge would barbeque our spareribs in oil if we brought a murder or arson charge against Whitey.'

'They planned ahead, didn't they?' Mace said, crestfallen.'I'll bet he has been playing cards every time there's been a case of vandalism reported in the valley.'

'I can't very well charge Havelock or anyone on his crew on the evidence of one set of bootprints.'

'I know, Sheriff. I'm not blaming you, only wondering how we're going to stop a major slaughter of my farmers. If people start to thinking they can kill someone and not be held accountable, there won't be anything to stop them from killing every Chinese farmer in the valley.'

'You have to let me handle this, Banyon. It's my job.'

'I know your capable, Wilcox,' Mace said, to pacify him. 'But you have to know, when the fight comes, these men will kill you. You're going to need help.'

'I'm going to need proof too.'

'If you can't get it, I will,' Mace told him. 'One weak link is all we need. Find the man who will break and the chain will not hold.'

The sheriff stood up. 'Like I said, let me handle this. I'm still the law in Oasis.'

Mace let him walk away without offering another word. He hated allowing a killer to walk free, or the man who hired him to hide behind a curtain of respectability. He paid for the meal and left the cafe. As he turned down the alley toward the livery stable, a man came out of the shadows. It was Whitey, poised in a gunman's crouch, his hand hovering over his gun!

'You were a big man in Kansas, Banyon, always hiding behind a badge.' He snorted his contempt. 'Well, I ain't impressed one little bit.'

Mace eased his hand to the hammer of his gun and slipped the tong off slowly, watching Whitey's every move. He was lean and appeared agile. His fair hair was as pale as new fallen snow – hence the name Whitey. His colorful, expensive, and quite narrow boots were newly shined, and he wore cow-puncher jeans and a cotton shirt. Only his gun tied low on his hip revealed his passion for the weapon.

'You killed Ti Fat,' Mace accused. 'I recognized your bootprints – both at the Wilcox place and where you set the fire on the Paxton spread last night.'

Whitey looked instinctively at his feet. 'I was afraid these special-made boots might give me away some day, but I never figured it would be from the prints I left.'

'You're feet are as narrow as most women.'

'Odd you can say that when you're around some of those – what do they call Chinese women – dainty feet?' He laughed. 'Bind their feet during their growing years so they don't have big feet. I'll bet you haven't got a single Chinese gal on your place with feet as big as mine.'

'OK,' Mace replied, not having known that tidbit of information. 'But it wasn't a woman doing the crimes around the valley, it was you.'

'Too bad you won't live to try and prove it, Banyon. Your time has run out.'

Mace set himself, every nerve tingling, his heart hammering wildly in his chest – likely at the prospect of having an ounce of lead about to pass through it. He blocked out every sound, sight and thought but the man facing him.

'So long, Banyon,' Whitey sneered haughtily. 'It's been … ' Then he grabbed for his gun!

Mace had anticipated the draw at the same instant. His reaction was automatic, from hours of practice, cocking back the hammer as the pistol cleared the holster, shooting from the hip from the necessity of being too close to miss and lacking time to aim. The two guns went off simultaneously.

Something burned a streak of fire along his ribs, as he fired a second time.

Whitey caught Mace's first bullet near his hip, the impact turning his body just enough that he missed his shot. As he tried to bring the gun around for a better shot, the second slug struck him in the chest. The jolt knocked the gun out of his hand and he staggered backwards, both hands drawn up to cover the mortal wound he'd received.

A look of utter amazement crossed his pained face. Whitey tried to mouth a word, but no sound reached his lips. His eyes closed, his mouth went slack, and he slumped to the ground in a heap. The man had committed his last crime and killed his last man.

'Hold it right there!' an icy voice warned Mace.

Looking in the direction of the challenge, Renz had a gun in his hand, pointed at Mace. Even as he lowered his weapon, Wilcox came running up the street towards them. Several other people gathered about to see what had happened.

'You even blink, Banyon,' Renz warned, 'and I'll kill you!'

Mace lowered his gun slowly and replaced it in his holster. He was not going to do anything stupid. It would have been exactly what Renz wanted.

'What happened?' the sheriff panted, looking at the downed gunman.

'I seen it all.' Renz spoke up before anyone else could speak. 'Banyon here came up behind Whitey – had his gun on him – and then, when Whitey turned around, he shot him. Whitey managed to get his gun out and fire a shot before Banyon finished him off, but he never had a chance.'

'You ought to fertilize fields at one of the farms, Renz. You're full of the stuff needed to make the crops grow.'

'What are you waiting for, Wilcox?' Renz yelped. 'I told you – I seen it happen. Banyon killed him without giving him a chance. Do your damn job!'

'I better have your gun, Banyon,' Wilcox said, reaching out with an open hand.

'Listen to me, Sheriff,' Mace said. 'I've arrested over a hundred men ... and killed several in the line of duty. If I'd have wanted to kill Whitey, I wouldn't have shot him first in the hip and gotten shot myself!'

'Let's do this right,' Wilcox maintained. 'Give me your gun and we will let the judge decide if the shooting was square or not.'

There was little Mace could do, unless he wanted to take on both the sheriff and Renz. He handed his gun to him and started up the street, walking toward the jail.

'Did you want him that bad?' Wilcox asked. 'I told you, we needed time and proof. What's the idea of bracing him in the street?'

'He's the one who confronted me, Wilcox. I had no idea he had come around the cafe to catch me on the livery side. If you recall, I didn't go with you to try and arrest him, so I didn't know where he was at.'

'Where's your witnesses?'

'Whitey didn't want anyone seeing him push me into a fight. He could have claimed anything after he killed me. Turns out, he wasn't any faster than me and I got off a lucky shot. Otherwise, you would be hauling him to jail.' He paused. 'Oh, wait a minute! I forgot. You don't arrest guilty men in this town.'

The sheriff's face darkened at the insult. It was a cheap shot, seeing as how Whitey had an alibi arranged ahead of time. Still, it stank ... being hauled off to jail for being forced to defend himself.

***

Havelock joined his wife at the window of the bank. In his office, he had barely heard the shots. Now he was looking out at the street because Lori seemed concerned about whatever was going on.

'What's happened?'

Lori moved away from him at once. 'Let your pet gunman tell you. He's coming this way.'

Seth grit his teeth, wondering how long Lori would continue to sink her spurs into his hide. She had been fighting him every step of the way, ever since Banyon arrived. He was beginning to wonder if she'd ever let up. She minded him, did what she was told, but there was no warmth in her body for him, and her looks were enough to chill a snowman.

Renz opened the door of the bank and looked around. Seeing there was no one in the room except for Lori and Seth, he tossed his hat on a vacant chair and took a seat.

'What happened out there, Renz? Why is Wilcox herding Banyon to jail?'

Renz was miffed and it showed. 'That rotten skunk just killed Whitey.'

'What?' Seth roared. 'I told Whitey to stay away from him!'

'Yeah, well he never was much for following orders. He slipped around the building and came in on Banyon's blind side. It should have been the end of Mace Banyon.' He swore. 'But Mace said Whitey gave him an even draw. Stupid clod, he always thought of himself as a fast gun. Well, he proved he was as fast as Banyon, but not as good a shot.'

'I don't believe it.'

'Check with the carpenter,' Renz sniped. 'He can show you the bullet holes.'

'What about Banyon?'

'I told Wilcox the Chinese lover is the one who started the fight – took Whitey from behind.'

'You think your testimony will be enough to convict him?'

'Judge Morrison don't care for gunplay on the streets of any town. He might swallow the story, but Banyon has been before judges before. He has a reputation and a history that might counter my testimony.'

Seth rubbed his hands together. 'We could sure stand to be rid of that ex-marshal.'

'I told you I should do it on my own.' Renz swore again, not paying any attention to Lori, who flinched from his vulgar profanity.

'Hard to believe he beat Whitey,' Seth said.

'Tell me about it. Bruno should have beaten the man to death, but failed. I still have to wonder how Banyon didn't bust up his hands in that fight. He should have been as slow getting his gun out as a librarian!'

'What's done is done,' Seth muttered. 'We've got to get rid of Banyon any way we can. He's a danger to us until he's locked away or dead and buried.'

'OK, boss, I'm with you. My testimony ought to put *him* behind bars – instead of him trying to put us there.'

Lori listened to the men's chatter without appearing interested. Banyon had been lucky to escape death, but could he escape the hangman's noose? She was a witness, as well as the lying Renz, but to open her mouth might mean her own death.

She knew nothing meant more to Seth than this land deal. He claimed that, once he had control of the bottomland side of the valley, he could sell it for a fortune. He would take her to a big city and they would live like royalty. It had sounded nice at the time, but it was different now. She had seen the Chinese farmers being harassed and beaten. Ti Fat had been brutally murdered and even Rodney – who was supposed to their friend – even his family had been victims of Seth's obsession. With Mace Banyon gone, Renz and other men like him would terrorize and drive out the Chinese farmers. Temple would be forced to sell the land for whatever Seth would pay.

Renz left the bank and Seth returned to his office. It left Lori alone with her thoughts, images and notions about the upcoming war. Banyon was a decent man, trying to protect the lawful rights of his farmers. Even Rodney had come around to his way of thinking. That gave her pause.

As if on cue, Rodney Paxton and Tincup appeared on their horses. They would do something to help Banyon. After all, he was an ex-marshal, respected and feared by the outlaws who knew him. And Rodney's backing would add to his credibility. Kemph, from the general store walked out to talk to the two men, so they would quickly learn what had transpired.

She saw Rodney look at the bank and could feel his eyes searching for a glimpse of her. She was not blind. There was a distant yearning in the attention he gave her. She was out of reach, being a married woman, but she knew, if something happened to Seth, she could turn to him. His was a desperate, hopeless kind of love, the kind that could never be expressed. It was morally wrong to covert a married woman, so he would never act on the emotions he felt. The reason she knew how the man felt – she suffered the same immoral feelings for him!

Chapter Nine

Banyon had explained each step taken with Whitey for the third time, when the door opened to the sheriff's office. Tincup and Rodney entered the jail, both of them puffed up with righteous indignation.

'What the hell, Wilcox?' Tincup wasted no words in greeting. 'You can't arrest Banyon.'

'The law states I have to arrest him until there's a hearing,' Wilcox argued. 'The only witness saw him approach Whitey from behind and start shooting.'

'That's a load of road-apples, and you know it!' Tincup pointed a finger at his chest. 'Kemph told me he saw Renz hurry past his store window *after* the shots were fired! Ain't no way he could have seen what happened around to the side of the building. About the only window facing that direction is the one over at the bank.'

'If Kemph will testify at the hearing, it should win Banyon's freedom,' Wilcox said. 'Still, I have to hold him until the judge hears the case.'

Tincup snorted sarcastically. 'Kemph won't dare open his mouth. Havelock has the deed to his store!'

'This is great,' Rodney said thickly. 'Whitey kills Ti Fat and sets fire to our place, and you put the only man in the valley who stands against Havelock in jail.'

'Whitey did admit to murdering Ti Fat,' Mace chipped in from his cell. 'He wondered how we had zeroed in on him as the killer. Of course, he only confessed to it because he was confident he could beat me to the draw.'

'There's blood on your shirt,' Tincup noticed, looking closer at Mace. 'You get hit?'

'Turns out, Whitey was every bit as fast as me. His shot was a couple inches off the mark – put a crease across my ribs.'

'You get the doctor over here right now!' Tincup barked the order at Wilcox. 'You put a man in jail, you better darn-tootin' see he's taken care of!'

'I'll see to it,' the sheriff said wearily. 'You men aren't making my job any easier, you know?'

'What I know is,' Rodney broke into the conversation, 'without Banyon to protect them, those Chinese farmers are all going to be targets. That means you have to protect them, Sheriff.'

'What am I supposed to do? I can't be every place at once.'

'Havelock is going to stir up a mob and try to run those people out of the valley. With this drought, there are a lot of jealous farmers looking to blame someone besides Nature. And our place is likely to be hit too.'

"Judge Morrison will be here in a few days. I sent a wire about Ti Fat being killed, so he already scheduled a trip here. Banyon can have his say and, hopefully, we'll get someone to back up his story about the gunfight.'

Rod said, 'And if not, you're willing to let him be railroaded into the hoosegow or a noose!'

'What about the protection of my farmers?" Tincup wanted to know. 'How are you going to guard a prisoner and stop the violence against them?'

'I'll have to hire a temporary deputy.'

Tincup laughed at the notion. 'Right. I can see the men lining up to take our side against Havelock and the rest of the valley.'

'In that case, how about you volunteer for the job?'

'Me?' Tincup's voice squeaked with his high-pitched disbelief.

'You could guard the prisoner. Banyon isn't going to pull any stunts with you here, and you won't let him go because you're too honest.'

'Thought this all out, have you?'

Wilcox grinned. 'I could ask Renz or Bruno to accept the job.'

Tincup sighed in defeat. 'Don't see how I can watch over my people and guard him too, but I'll do it.'

'What about me?' Rodney wanted to know. 'Give me one of those badges, so anyone I shoot trying to set fire to one of our fields – it'll be legal.'

Wilcox appeared uncertain. 'Some of these men are your friends, Paxton.'

'After Whitey burning one of our fields, I don't count Bruno or Renz as friends.'

'It could be dangerous,' Mace put in from his cell. 'You don't want to be involved in a shooting war.'

'There's a lot of farmers to keep watch over,' Rodney countered. 'I could help watch over the valley when Pa don't need me on the farm. If it comes to trouble, I owe a debt to some of those Chinese – our whole family owes them.'

'All right,' Wilcox agreed reluctantly. 'I hereby deputize you both.'

'Not without a badge and holding up my hand, you don't,' Tincup objected. 'I know the rules of becoming a deputy.'

'All right,' Wilcox sighed. 'Hold up your right hand and say: *I do.*' They did as directed and he opened a desk drawer and removed two deputy sheriff badges. He handed one to each of them without another word.

'I'd feel better about this,' Rodney said, 'if I thought the two of us together could handle either Bruno or Renz.'

'We ain't gotta choice now, sonny boy,' Tincup said. 'We's the law.'

Wilcox groaned. 'I know I'm going to regret this.'

***

Mace paced a path in his cell the next several days. Su Lee brought his meals, and Tincup kept him informed on everything that transpired. There was still no rain, but no attacks or trouble either. Evidently, Havelock had pulled back his bullies, keeping them in harness until after Judge Morrison's visit. They wanted a quiet town, with a lot of quiet people. With a combination of those two ingredients, Mace just might get sent to prison for a good long sentence. That or hanged. Either way, it didn't look good, because Renz was still the only witness to come forward.

The day the judge arrived, Wilcox was busy sweeping the floor. He watched the man get off the stage and put away his broom. Mace was able to see out the window as the sheriff left the office and intercepted the judge. As Wilcox pointed at the jail, Mace had little doubt he was the subject being discussed.

An hour later, Tincup and Rodney took Mace out of his cell. They led him across the street to the biggest saloon in town. It was supposed to be a closed hearing, but there were a number of people in attendance, including Havelock, his wife, and several Chinese.

Judge Morrison was a heavyset man, with frigid dark eyes, coal-black hair, and a voice as deep as a bullfrog's. He could boom his words over the noise of a crowd, and he was notorious for dealing out tough sentences. In his black robe, he looked ominous.

Mace took a chair at the front of the room, the judge having put a desk on the platform that was occasionally used for traveling shows or entertainment. He was able to look down on the crowd that way, adding to his air of superiority.

After a few words of greeting and explanation as to his purpose, the judge banged his gavel on the desk.

'First order of business is the death of the man called Ti Fat. Sheriff, would you state the facts surrounding this case?'

Wilcox testified as to what had taken place. He was followed by the town doctor, who expounded on the injuries suffered by the young man. Also brought up were the recent attacks on livestock, the theft and vandalism, and finally the fire at the Paxton place.

'It is obvious to the court,' Morrison announced, once he had collect the information, 'that Ti Fat was harassing the neighboring farms. I must conclude the fellow was caught in the act, beaten for his misdeeds and died of his injuries. Therefore I find no reason to pursue – '

'If you'll pardon the interruption, Judge,' Mace spoke up, standing to make his voice heard. 'There is no proof whatsoever that Ti Fat was anything other than a victim of violence against one of my farmers. Ed Paxton and I discovered the ruse of a Chinese man doing the mischief by proving the culprit was the criminal known as Whitey Curn!'

'Ah, yes, the marvelous detective work Sheriff Wilcox spoke of – a pair of unusually narrow boots,' the judge declared with disdain. 'Hardly a case that would stand up in a court of law.'

'The man admitted his guilt to me, when he forced me into a gunfight.'

Judge Morrison glared down at him. 'We will commence determining your guilt concerning Whitey Curn in due course. Sit down and be silent in the court.'

Mace held his tongue, but knew the dismissal of Ti Fat's death would virtually open the door to violence on his farmers. If Havelock's men could kill with impunity, how could you defend the Chinese?

'Moving on,' Morrison said, eying Mace with disfavor, 'the second case to be heard is a preliminary hearing concerning the death of the aforementioned Whitey Curn.' The judge paused to look over the paperwork Wilcox had provided. He didn't appear all that interested.

'Mace Banyon, do you deny killing Mr. Curn?'

'He forced the fight, after he confessed his crimes – which you have chosen to ignore,' Mace explained. 'We both fired at the same time, but mine was the better shot. I killed him with my second bullet to prevent him from doing the same to me.' With a trace of ire, he added: 'The law has a name for that – it's known as *Self-defense*!'

Morrison frowned his displeasure. 'I'm aware of your past history, Mr Banyon. As an ex-officer of the law, I think you look at self-defense differently than most. When you are making an arrest, no one expects you to wait for the accused to draw his gun first. It is, however, a completely different story when you are a private citizen.'

'I wasn't prepared for this fight, and I didn't go looking for it. Whitey accosted me and forced the gunfight. He was afraid I'd find enough evidence to link him to Ti Fat's murder. He didn't want me doing any more snooping.'

'That isn't what the witness claims.'

Mace glanced over at Renz. 'The witness wasn't even there at the time. He arrived after the fight was over. Plus, he works for the same crook as Whitey Curn.'

The judge swung his attention to Renz. 'What do you say to that, Mr Renz?'

'He's lying to save his neck, Judge. I saw the whole thing. He come up behind Whitey with his gun out. He shot Whitey before he had a chance to defend himself. Too bad Whitey didn't get off a better shot.'

Morrison gave Mace another distasteful look. 'With no evidence to support your story, Mr Banyon, I am going to direct this case go to trial. The charge will be murder.'

'Your honor?' a feminine voice suddenly spoke up.

Mace turned in his chair, surprised to see Lori Havelock was standing up. Seth's own expression was one of suppressed rage, his face literally black with controlled fury.

'Do you have something to add to this hearing, madam?'

'I also witnessed the shoot-out between Mr Banyon and Whitey Curn. I happened to be at the bank window and saw the whole thing.'

'So you can collaborate what Mr Renz has said?' the judge inquired.

She let her eyes drift to the lean gunman. A wisp of a smile flew across her lips like a fleeting shadow. 'As Mr Banyon has told you, Mr Renz works for my husband. I couldn't hear the words that passed between them, but Mr Curn was the one who initiated the fight. He stepped out in front of Mace Banyon and stopped him from going to the livery. The two of them pulled their guns at precisely the same instant. It was so quick I could hardly see it, but both guns went off so closely to the same time, it sounded like a single shot. Mr Banyon recovered first and fired a second time, killing Mr Curn. It was quite obvious that Whitey forced the fight, not Mr Banyon.'

The judge looked back at Renz. The man's face was flushed with embarrassment and anger, but he could hardly call the wife of his boss a liar.

'Do you care to amend your testimony, Mr Renz?' Morrison asked, a cool note in his tone.

'I ... I got there right after the shooting,' he muttered, almost too softly to be heard. 'My story – I said what I figured had happened, because I thought Whitey was faster with a gun than Banyon. I suppose it might have happened the way Mrs Havelock says.'

'In view of such testimony, I am reversing my decision. The finding if Self-defense, Mr Banyon.' He still regarded him with an icy stare. 'But I will be watching for any trouble out of you in the future.'

Mace couldn't imagine the trouble Mrs Havelock was going to be in. He would have to do something to protect her ... though he had no idea as to what or how. He put his own granite gaze on the judge.

'As a country, Judge, all Americans are entitled to the benefits of our laws. Being Chinese is not a crime, nor should the murder of an innocent man like Ti Fat be discarded because of the influence held by money and power. There is a lot of hostility towards my farmers, not because they are Chinese, but because we have the best farmland in the country. I would expect my workers to be given the same courtesy and protection as any other American citizen.'

'I find no problem with your speech, Mr Banyon. But if it comes to shooting and killing, there will be repercussions.'

'So long as they apply equally under the law,' Mace replied. 'It's all I ask ... and it's something I must insist on.'

'This hearing is adjourned,' Morrison said, banging his gavel down once more.

Mace walked past the greeting hands of Tincup and Rodney Paxton, stopping at the table where Seth and Lori Havelock were sitting. With his hat in his hand, he addressed the young lady.

'I'm obliged to you, Mrs Havelock, for having the courage to tell the truth today.'

Lori had only given his approach an offhand attention, but as Rodney came up to stand alongside Mace, a pink hue entered her cheeks. She cleared her throat before speaking.

'I felt it was my Christian duty, Mr Banyon. There was nothing personal about it.'

'Thank you all the same,' he said. Then he put an admonitory look on Seth.

'I hope you share your wife's moral attributes, Mr Havelock. If you should decide to harm her in any way for her testimony, I'd take it personally. You might even say I would be compelled to retaliate.'

'Don't you threaten me!' Havelock barked, boiling just beneath the surface. 'Lori is my wife and I'll treat her as I see fit.'

'Just so you see fit to treat her decent, Havelock. I'm not the kind of man who makes idle threats – I make promises.' He smiled a wry smile. 'And I always keep my promises.'

'The same goes for me,' Rodney spoke up. 'I'd be real put out if any harm came to a lady who had the fortitude to tell the truth.'

'I don't take pushing from anyone!' Seth warned.

'It's not pushing,' Mace corrected him. 'We are concerned citizens, expressing our gratitude to your wife for her courage. If you want to make more of it than that, Rodney and I are at your immediate disposal.'

'Your time will come soon enough,' Havelock warned them both. He stood up, yanked Lori to her feet, and stormed from the room. Renz watched them leave and moved over to pause in front of Mace.

'I'll be keeping an eye on you, Banyon. I might not have seen you draw, but I'm a lot quicker than Whitey. He only thought he was good ... I don't have any doubt.'

'There's no reason I should test your claim, unless you cross the line. You leave my workers be, and we'll get along all right.'

The gunman laughed, a mocking sort of snicker. 'I follow my orders, Banyon. If I'm ordered to kill you, I'll get the job done.'

'A faster gun doesn't always win the fight, Renz. You can check with some of those I've sent to prison or boot hill.'

Renz eyed Mace a moment longer, then wandered out of the saloon. There was no fear in the man, for he had every confidence that he was better with a gun than Mace.

Unfortunately, Mace shared the same feeling.

Chapter Ten

Tong, Su Lee, and a new visitor to the house, Liu Yung, were all in the large sitting room at the main house.

Mace and Tincup were seated on a couch, while the other three sat across from them on chairs. Each had their own thoughts, both sides uncomfortable about how to converse about the loss of Ti Fat.

'We know you did what you could,' Su Lee spoke to Mace, breaking the long silence. 'You have avenged Ti Fat's death by killing Whitey Curn.'

'But Whitey wasn't judged guilty,' Tincup complained. 'Morrison wouldn't even listen to our arguments.'

'We are satisfied that you did all within your power. This land does not look with favor on the Chinese people. We understand many in the valley resent us, and the judge had only your word of Whitey Curn's confession.'

'Everyone is supposed to have equal justice – red, white or green. However, Morrison didn't have any evidence, other than a boot print and my word,' Mace clarified. 'It wasn't sufficient proof.'

'We are happy they didn't decide to hang you for the gunman's death.'

'Morrison likely gave it some thought. Vigilantes are not well thought of by the judicial class, fearing innocent people might be killed. If Mrs Havelock had not spoken up, I would be facing a trial.'

'Thing is,' Tincup got around to the upcoming trouble, 'it might take a fight to keep our land and farms intact. Havelock is bound to try and drive us out.'

'This land is our own,' Tong said. 'Many of the workers have ... ' He looked at Su Lee, unable to think of the words.

'There are some who have earned more than half of price of their land,' she expounded. 'In several more years, all of the Chinese will own the property they are working.'

'I've seen the figures in the account book,' Mace said. 'But, my point is, it might mean a fight to keep your farms.'

Su Lee replied: 'Growing up, father told me he was appalled by the incredible savagery of this land, of some of the harsh men who lived and died. There were fights over gold, over land, and even over women. When we followed the railroad, many of our people died from accidents and cave-ins. It was the price of westward progress. My father and those like him did their jobs, even when it meant risking death. It is the way of the Chinese, willing to work for lower wages and without complaint.'

'I was there too, Su Lee,' Tincup reminded her. 'Your father and all of the men working the land here deserve a chance at a better life. Mr Temple has offered them that life – a home of their own. What Mace and I are saying, if this comes to a fight, we might need everyone to stand up against Havelock's men and maybe even the people in town – whatever it takes.' He eyed his old friend. 'Tong, can they do that? Can they take up weapons and defend this side of the valley?'

'We will endure,' he said, the meaning vague. 'As for our life here: one life has ended, but a new life is begun. Su Lee and Liu Yung will marry Sunday. We ask you to join us.'

'Thank you, Tong,' Mace replied. 'We would be honored.'

Tong rose from his place in the room. 'Come, Su Lee, it is time to sleep.'

Liu also rose, in respect for the old man. He bowed his departing farewell, and the three of them left the main sitting room together.

'I admire those folks,' Tincup remarked once they were out of earshot.

'There's a great deal to be said for their culture,' Mace agreed. 'Especially their desire for a peaceful existence.'

'What I admire is the respect they have for the old folks. Over here, most people simply forget or ignore us old-timers. They seem to think getting gray hair means everything you've learned during your life don't mean squat. The Chinese are just the opposite. As they get older, they gain more respect. The young listen to their advice, follow their decisions and treat them decent.'

'It's a commendable society, all right.'

'When you get to be my age, Banyon, it's downright extraordinary. I wish I had me some kids who would worry when I get to the point where my body fails me and I can't get around. I got nobody in the world who gives a hoot if I live or die.'

'You've got me ... until I walk into a bullet,' Mace affirmed. 'Besides, you don't seem all that old.'

'No? I'm pushing sixty.'

Mace blinked at the declaration.' Sixty? Seriously?'

'Well, in my mid-fifties anyhow. I'm not real certain when I was born – too young to remember at the time. But I've climbed a hill or two the past forty years.'

'Shucks, Tincup, you ought to be looking for a soft job to retire with, instead of sticking your neck out in this game. As a man gets along in years, he needs peace and quiet, lots of hours in the sun contemplating or fishing at his favorite water hole.'

'You trying to bury me?' Tincup piped up, his voice an octave higher.

'Just saying,' Mace said with a grin. 'A fellow as old and crotchety as you, he ought to find a peaceful little corner and curl up with a good book. No need risking his life in a fight against overwhelming odds.'

'I don't need no nursemaid looking after me!' Tincup alleged hotly. 'I'll carry my weight right to the grave. By gad-fry! I'll even walk to the hole and dig it myself! You think because I've got a couple gray hairs and couldn't whip Bruno in a fist-fight that I'm over the hill and past my prime, do you?'

'I don't recall starting this conversation,' Mace countered defensively. 'You're the one who brought up age.'

'Well, you best let it lie, or I'll have to show you just how tough I can be!'

'Whatever you say, Tincup.'

'You should get some sleep,' he told Mace. 'You young whippersnappers need more time in the sack than us more mature people.'

Mace chuckled under his breath. 'I am feeling a little worn out. Didn't get much sleep behind bars. All that time lying around, but saw visions of being hanged every time I closed my eyes. You probably need a little sleep yourself.'

'Bah! I've worked at jobs where we only got sleep one night a week, and that was pulling guard duty at the same time. You youngsters are all alike – soft!'

'Story like that, and you wonder why young people don't ask your advice.'

The man chuckled. 'I may be given to ... what's the word – *exaggerate* some from time to time.'

'I'm glad to know your on my side, Tincup.'

'See you in the morning,' he said.

Mace headed off to his bedroom, but his thoughts were still on the day's events. Havelock was not going to take defeat lying down. He would surely start trouble again, and soon.

***

Rodney Paxton had been struck by the same notion, standing in the shadows, keeping watch on the Havelock place. Renz had gone into the main house earlier, but it seemed quiet. They were sure to be planning their next move.

His curiosity wasn't only for what evil deeds those two might conjure up. He was sticking close enough to respond if Lori should cry out. She had stuck her neck out for Banyon, and Seth was not a forgiving man. If he got rough with her ….

It was awkward, feeling the tightness in his chest each time she entered his thoughts. The woman was married to another man, and to even daydream of her in a romantic light was wrong. Rodney shook his head, but the lady continued to plague him.

He liked the way Lori walked, the slight tilt of her head when she knew he was watching. She often avoided looking in his direction, and that alone made him aware that she knew he was there. It was a childish game, but they played it frequently. Whenever she spoke to him, it was businesslike, but her eyes could not hide her own clandestine desires. She was stuck in a loveless marriage, one she had been forced into. Was is so wrong for them to have a mutual fantasy, to wonder what their lives could have been?

Bruno appeared in the yard and entered the house. This was a serious meeting, with Havelock bringing in his two thugs to plan their next action. How Rodney wished he dared sneak up to the house and listen at a window. But, to be caught eavesdropping would mean more than a beating, it would be the start of a war.

Considering Lori was in the house, he wondered if she would overhear their plans. If he could get her alone for a moment or two ….

The idea stirred the familiar surreptitious yearning. Somehow, for the sake of the Chinese and his family, he had to manage it. He knew Lori would confide in him. Banyon and he needed to be ready for anything, and she was the only spy they had.

He would try the next morning. He knew Seth left for the bank a few minutes or an hour ahead of her. His routine was to look over the books, double-check the funds on hand, and count out the cash drawer, all before the bank opened for business. Lori ran the window as teller, but he was careful about allowing her freedom of access to his money. She didn't have to be there as long as the doors were locked. It might give him the few moments he needed.

***

Mace was seated at the breakfast table when Rodney arrived at his house. Su Lee prepared several extra eggs and added a slice of ham to the griddle. Rodney thanked both Mace and Su Lee, and took a chair at the table. As they ate, they discussed the situation.

'So you spoke to Lori this morning?'

'Yes. Seth went to work at his usual time and I saw both Bruno and Renz eating breakfast at the cafe.'

'How did she look? Do you think Seth knocked her around at all?'

'No,' Rodney did not hide his puzzlement. 'In fact, she said he took the whole thing in stride, not even cussing her out for betraying him. However, I'm sure he no longer trusts her.'

'If Bruno and Renz stayed late,' Mace repeated what he had told him, 'It can't be good for us.'

'It was nearly midnight when they left the house. I watched them until they went to bed at the bunkhouse. Whatever they came up with, it wasn't happening right away.'

'No rain again today, so they might plan to use a mob for any action against us.'

'Tonight would be a good night,' Rodney said. 'It's Saturday and many of the farmers will be in town to drink away their worries about the drought. A little free whiskey, someone planted to start in about how good our family and the Chinese farmers have it – wouldn't take much more than that to start a riot.'

'It's a likely plan of action,' Mace concurred.

'What do you suggest?' Rodney asked. 'I know you're more experienced at this sort of thing than the rest of us.'

'Mobs are the worst to deal with,' Mace said. 'A person can be reasoned with – well, most of them. But a mob has no reason, no sanity; they act on impulse, emotion, passion. If you don't stop the leaders and knock them down hard, the mob will run wild and do things none of those people would have thought about doing on their own.'

'Sounds like we're in for a real storm.'

'First off, get Wilcox involved,' Mace told Rodney. 'Have him be ready to move in and put a halt to any talk that will spur the mob. If he has any men he can trust, he needs to have them at his side.'

'And if that doesn't work?'

'Then it's you, me and Tincup against the rest of the valley.'

'Ouch!' Rodney said. 'Those are powerful odds.'

Mace grinned. 'Better than you alone at your place or me and Tincup at ours.'

Rodney's grim expression cracked into a smile. 'Dad-gum, you paint one rosy picture, Banyon. I can see why you didn't get promoted to an actual U. S. Marshal. You're a rotten motivator.'

'Yeah, I tried being optimistic twice I can remember -- and reality knocked me on my can both times.'

'Never thought about you being an educated man,' Rodney said. 'But you use words one hardly ever hears – *optimistic, reality*. Sounds impressive.'

'My mother wanted me to go to college. She thought I might amount to something.' Mace laughed. 'She'd roll over in her grave if she knew what I've done the past few years.'

'And your dad?'

'He died in the war at Gettysburg. We ended up living with Mom's folks until I was old enough to get out on my own.'

'OK, it's nice to know I'm working with a literate man. Might want to write something nice for Wilcox to say over our graves.'

'You coming to the wedding for Su Lee Sunday?' Mace asked, changing the subject.

'I reckon so. Mercy has been fussing with her best dress all week long – ever since Tong gave us the invite. I ain't much for dressing up, but I do have a Sunday go-to-meeting suit.'

Mace walked out with Rodney and saw him off, then Tong was there with a saddled horse for him. He thanked the man and headed to the farms that were most affected by the drought.

He spent most of the day trying to talk to the farmers. Some were cordial, some were hostile, and all of them resented Temple controlling the best land in the valley. As a whole, they were unhappy, worried and concerned the rain wouldn't get there in time to save their crops.

He sympathized with their plight, but made it clear that Temple – not the Chinese sharecroppers – held title to the bottomlands. Any complaints about his farmers, needed to be directed to Mace and not acted upon in anger.

For the most part, he figured he had wasted the day and his breath. The dry farmers knew that the irrigated fields were green and thriving, while their own plants turned brown and wilted under the sun.

Preparing for Saturday night, Mace felt a foreboding, an inner dread of what might take place. He cleaned and oiled his six-gun, then did the same with his rifle. Tincup had his shotgun ready, but had admitted it would be difficult to open up on a mob with it.

'The thing is,' he told Mace at supper, 'some of these men are friends of mine. I hate the idea that I might end up shooting at one of them.'

'We will not fire except as a last resort to save lives and property, Tincup. A mob has no conscience and they aren't friends and neighbors when they are rioting. In the heat of action, they turn into a pack of wolves, ripping and tearing, destroying and killing. If all else fails, we'll have to use force.'

'Sure. Sixty farmers against three or four of us. You know which side using force will be stronger.'

'I talked a few of them into staying home tonight ... I hope.'

'There's word of a private party for a number of them – over at the Dry Wash Saloon,' Tincup said. 'Going to be Havelock's treat. Drinks all around and enough of that snake juice will incite them to action against us.'

'Havelock is desperate. He knows a good rain will turn the people's mood and they will be happy with their lives again. He has to use this dry period, before the rain comes.'

'How do we prepare ourselves?' Tincup wanted to know.

'Keep an eye on things and keep our guns handy. If they come looking for trouble, we need to stop them before they get rolling. If we're too late or fail, they might sweep across the valley and destroy every farm and every building we have.'

Tincup scratched his head. 'I sure hope I'm around to attend Su's wedding tomorrow.'

'Me too, Tincup. Me too.'

Chapter Eleven

Havelock surveyed the men sitting at the saloon tables. They were in a depressed, ugly mood. Renz had been riling them for fifteen minutes about the murder of Whitey Curn. Suddenly, after the arrival of Mace Banyon, Renz had become one of the dry farmers, one of the boys.

It mattered not that Bruno, Renz and Whitey had been bullies, making certain that Seth got his money on time and harassing them when they were a day late. Now, with Banyon to take the heat, and him being a Chinese sympathizer, Renz was on their side. Feeling the time was right, Seth stood up in the center of the room. All fell quiet before him.

'It seems to me,' he began, using his booming voice, 'that the time has come for action!'

Seth grinned inwardly at the grumbling approval, then continued. 'I have nothing personal against the Chinese, not from a human standpoint. They mind their own affairs, tend pretty much to themselves, and stay to their side of town. The trouble is, they will soon own the whole town!'

That brought an angry roar of agreement. He waited while some men swore oaths and voiced their personal complaints, before holding up his hands to silence the group once more.

'What I'm getting at is this,' he said harshly. 'The Chinese have the best growing soil in the valley. They make a lot of money, but they only spend it in the Chinese stores. Some of them send their money home to China so it leaves the country forever. As far as civic improvements, they don't contribute one blessed thing towards helping our town prosper. Their farms grow fat and rich, while your crops wither and die.

'Now I ask you, does that land company care? Do you see Silas Temple sending some of his profits to help benefit the rest of the valley, or financing the building of a dam so that more of you could irrigate your fields?'

He let a roar of men answer loudly, then put a sneer on his lips. 'No! He sends a gunman to kill anyone who questions the worth of the Chinese to our community!'

Those words raised the noise level to the rafters, inebriated men all shouting curses and oaths against Banyon and the Chinese. They were tired of working their bodies to the point of exhaustion and still watching their crops perish. Even in a good year, the Chinese farms made two or three-times as much with their crop sales as they did. With the damnable drought, they wanted someone to blame, someone they could strike at, other than Nature itself. The lone outlet for their wrath was Banyon and his Chinese farmers.

'I say to you men,' Havelock went on, 'that unless something is done, we'll all dry up and die like your fields. My money is gone, lent out to you year after year, trying to help make this a prosperous valley. If you go under, so do I. Kemph and the other businessmen are in the same shape, for it's your money that keeps us all going. The Chinese offer us nothing ... not one dime of their money! Even this saloon will collapse without your financial help. How much longer can we last, men? A week? A month?'

There were vexed scowls, clenched fists being raise, the gnashing of teeth. These were bitter, angry, besotted men, looking for a release for their frustration and hate. Seth knew what he was doing, and just how far he could push them.

'I say we drive the slant-eyed devils out of the country – including the Chinese lovers, Banyon and the Paxtons!'

'We can start right here in town!' Renz cried, pulling his gun. He raised it over his head and led the charge for the door.

Sheriff Wilcox had gotten there after hearing the shouts over at the jail. He tried to get in front of the saloon exit, but Renz rammed into him, knocking him to the ground. Before he could get his feet under him, someone clouted him on the head, and the crowd trampled over him, leaving the sheriff unconscious in the middle of the street.

***

Mace heard a cry of alarm and hurried to the front door of his house. He saw a small Chinese man running towards him, his arms waving in fright.

'Fai-loy! He shouted. 'Fai-loy!'

'What the Sam Hill does *fai-loy* mean?' he asked over his shoulder, as Tincup came from his room to join him.

'He wants us to come quick,' Tincup replied. 'Grab your gun! We've got trouble!'

Mace grabbed his rifle, and the two of them raced toward town. It was a couple hundred yards away, but the sounds of yelling and screams were audible.

'It's the Chinese district!' Tincup shouted.

They ran until they reached the main street. The Chinese general store and laundry were under assault by over a dozen men.

Rodney Paxton was standing off to one side. He had a shotgun in his hands and four adult Chinese and two children cowering behind him. The glass was breaking amongst the shouts and yells of the drunken group of men. The crash and bang of goods being thrown about could also be heard.

'I got these people out,' Rodney told Mace and Tincup. 'It'd be suicide for us to try and go in there and break them up. They've about destroyed the store and laundry anyhow.'

Mace hated to agree, but there were no less than thirty men involved. With Renz and Bruno among them, it would be difficult to prevent a slaughter on both sides.

'We can't stand by while they tear the town apart!' Tincup cried.

'We will draw a line between the businesses and the rest of the village,' Mace outlined. 'We have to keep them from destroying people's homes and maybe killing some of them.'

'Where's the sheriff?' Tincup asked Rodney, resigning himself to the fact that there was little else they could do.

'I saw him head for the saloon, right before the riot started. He must have gotten waylaid somewhere.'

'If they've hurt Wilcox, they've crossed the line from blowing off steam to being willing to kill innocent people,' Tincup proclaimed. 'First man to point a gun my way is gonna get a load of buckshot in his gizzard.'

No sooner had the words left his mouth than several men split off from the vandals. Mace had Tincup to his left, while Rodney was on his right. The Chinese took off down the street, hurrying to their homes. If they had to flee for their lives, they wanted to grab whatever they could before the mob arrived.

Mace let the men come, twelve to fifteen of them. When they got to within a hundred feet, he fired at their feet, blasting off three rapid shots. It halted the group, as most of them were carrying clubs or axes for tearing things up, not wielding rifles or guns.

'You men have done enough damage for one night!' Mace warned them. 'You've destroyed years of work for some decent, innocent people. That's as much as you're going to do.'

Renz headed the group, but a hundred feet was too far to be accurate with a handgun. He started to move forward, but Mace put a bullet between his feet and he stopped.

'The next shot won't be a warning,' Mace announced. 'Keep coming – any of you – and we'll drop you like the rabid animals you are acting like.'

'You can't protect your coolie pals, Banyon! We're going to drive them all out of the country!'

'I'll kill the first man who harms one of the Chinese or raises a hand to destroy their personal property.'

'They've got all the good land!' one of the farmers called out. 'You expect us to stand by and starve while they prosper?'

'The land isn't theirs,' Mace reminded him and the others. 'If Temple had hired white tenant farmers, you wouldn't think of trying to run them off. I'm telling you here and now that attacking the people under my charge will get you nothing but a belly full of lead.'

Renz took a single step forward, but no one followed the move – including Bruno, who was right beside him. The drink and exertion of destruction had taken a toll on the mob. Some of them were having second thoughts – looking down the barrels of three guns.

'You're going to push once too often, Banyon,' Renz threatened.

'I'm not the one doing the pushing – I'm standing up for what is right. If it wasn't for the drought, none of the farmers with you would be risking their lives on Havelock's say-so.'

'As deputy sheriff of Oasis,' Rodney called out. 'I'm telling you men to go home. Any man I recognize will be held accountable for the damage tonight. That means fines to pay for what you've destroyed and jail time if you resist.'

'I'm a deputy sheriff too, you drunken bunch of thugs!' Tincup confirmed. 'Go home and sleep off the free drinks from the greedy tyrant who has you blindly doing his bidding.'

Reluctantly, the group began to break up, some wandering off to main street and the saloon, while others headed for their homes.

Once the crowd was disbursed, Mace surveyed the damage in the store and laundry, while Tincup and Rodney went looking for the sheriff. Both businesses had little more than a framework left standing, with litter, broken shelves and damaged goods scattered all about. Dried fish and rice covered the floor of the store, and the stoves and shelving at the laundry had been trashed.

Rodney and Tincup helped the still-groggy Wilcox home to his wife. Then the three of them spent some time cleaning up some of the litter from the street in front of the shop and laundry. The proprietors would have their hands full putting their placed back in order, but at least no one had been injured or killed.

As they called it a night, Rodney said he would check the saloons and make certain the farmers had gone home.

Tincup shook his head in disgust. 'Hell of a way for grown men to act. Ain't one of those clod-hoppers who could have stood alongside Tong and me when we was laying rail.'

'This was a warning volley,' Mace said. 'The next time Seth turns Renz loose, there won't be any brakes.'

'When that happens, I reckon we'll get trampled over,' Tincup finished.

'You want to pack your gear and haul freight, I'll figure you're the smarter of us two.'

He grunted his contempt. 'I'm too old to start running and hiding every time some jack with a gun thinks he can tack my hide to a wall. Besides, Tong is like family. He's got no one else to stand up with him and his people.'

'We will meet whatever force comes our way with equal force,' Mace avowed. 'Let's just hope the farmers get a case of guilty conscience tomorrow at church.'

'I ain't worried about them,' Tincup said. 'Take away the drink and most of them will curse the weather, not the Chinese. It's Havelock we are going to have to deal with ... and soon.'

Chapter Twelve

Despite the turmoil and terror of the previous night, the wedding feast – outside the couple's new home – found most of the guests in a jovial mood. There was a minimum of Chinese decor, but the small house was brightly decorated all the same. So was a table that had been set outside for food and drink.

Su Lee was at the side of her new husband, positively beaming with her happiness. Liu Yung smiled a lot too, although he was obviously shy about the attention.

Mace found himself dawn to the side of Mercy Paxton, who was prettier than any picture in a yellow gown with white lace.

'You look like you belong in a garden,' Mace told her.

'Really?'

'You'd be the most beautiful flower blooming.'

She laughed. 'Mace Banyon, I didn't know you had a line of flattery.'

'It's a very short line,' he admitted. 'I haven't had much practice, and I hardly ever have a chance to talk to a pretty girl.'

'Explains why you're not married. Some lines have hooks attached – and usually, it's the lady holding the pole.'

'I haven't had to avoid being snared,' he reparteed. 'My choice of professions usually kept husband-seekers at bay.'

A demure smile lit up her already luminous features. 'And do you see me as one of those, a husband-seeker?'

'I 'spect most gals are looking for the right man, same as most men are searching for the right woman.'

'You strike me as a man who could be a good prospect, other than being a little too quick to get involved in someone else's troubles.'

'It's one of those things I heard a learned doctor say once – a personality flaw.'

She uttered a rather girlish giggle. 'Yes, I am in complete agreement.'

There was something fresh and innocent about the girl's candid gaze, and her honest mirth was musical and gay. Mace hoped his inner cravings were not reflected in his own gaze – he didn't wish to look like a lovesick puppy. To cover his yearning, he turned to the girl's history.

'I'm impressed by your sophistication, being so far from any schools of higher learning. Most girls I grew up around were fortunate if they learned to read and write. Most of the farmers I've come across don't even bother with that much, seeing as how the girls usually spend all of the time learning the crafts of their lifestyle – mending, sewing, cooking, cleaning – you know what I mean.'

There was something imbedded in the depths of her eyes, but Mace couldn't decipher what it meant. Mercy chose to follow his conversation.

'The reverend in town will teach anyone who wants to learn to read and write,' she said. 'He and Su Lee helped many of the Chinese to speak passable English, and he has a very nice library. I've borrowed many books from him. Are you worried because I don't have a farmyard drawl?'

He chuckled. 'It would sound out of place on your lips.'

'So,' she asked boldly, 'are you trying to court me or just pass the time with a young lady?'

Mace about choked on the question. 'Uh, like I said, I haven't spent a lot of time trying to woo a gal. I admit, you are refreshingly bright and easy to talk to. And, given the chance, I'd like nothing better than to take a long walk with you. I'd admire being able to enjoy the songs of the birds and see the sunshine reflecting from your hair.'

She turned serious. 'But we can't do that, can we.'

It wasn't a question. Mace heaved a sigh. 'Troubles don't allow a man time to do what he wants.'

'What about last night?' she asked. 'Rodney said he thought it might come to a gunfight, but you averted it.'

'That there's the right word – averted. It doesn't mean the end, because we know it was one more step towards a real war.'

'Because Havelock won't give up.'

'I'll have to cull the herd before they stampede. The banker is running the cattle, so it's him I am going to have to stop.'

'He still has Bruno and Renz.'

"I've got Tincup and Wilcox,' Mace countered. 'Rodney was at our side last night too, and him being a farmer helps.'

'I called on you after you fought with Bruno,' Mercy admitted. 'I asked Su Lee not to tell you, because you were sleeping.' She wrung her hands. 'You suffered such a beating, I worried you might have internal injuries.'

'I remember you telling me I won the fight.'

'I was relieved you had *survived* the fight.'

'It's not something I want to do again,' Mace admitted.

'With Renz, it will be for keeps!' she declared. 'He is deadly with a gun, much more so than Whitey.'

'I've dealt with men who were faster to get their gun out than me before,' he told her. 'If it comes to a fight, I'll figure out a way to even the odds.'

Mercy studied him with a candid scrutiny, seeking to determine if he was as confident as his statement.

'I wish I could be sure of that,' she said. 'If you're bravado is for my sake, please don't continue to mislead me.'

Mace felt warm under the collar and it had nothing to do with the sun. He noticed the feast had ended and everyone had gone into the house to offer gifts and congratulations. Only the two of them were left outside.

'I've been in some tight spots and always got out with a whole skin. Like I said, I've handled men like Renz before.' He grinned to lighten her mood. 'Does it matter so much?'

'It matters a great deal, Mace. If I fall in love with a man, I expect him to remain alive long enough to enjoy it.'

Her bluntness stunned him more than one of Bruno's roundhouse punches. He felt his mouth fall open and had to physically will himself to close it.

'Come on,' he put a teasing tone into is words, 'you could never fall for a loser like me.'

'No,' she quipped, 'I couldn't fall for a man *like* you. It would have to be you – and losing is not a viable option!'

'I don't understand, Mercy. I haven't yet had time to take you for a buggy ride, go on a picnic in the country, not even stomp all over your feet at a dance. We probably haven't been together for more than a few hours. You certainly don't think you … I mean we…'

'I believe I've had enough time to understand what kind of man you are,' Mercy replied carefully, as if choosing every word. 'And I was under the impression you were quite taken with me too.'

'That's calling a mountain a gopher mound, lady. I fell in love with you the first time I saw you under that wagon wheel. But – '

'If that's so, then why don't you show it? I can't believe I'm doing all of the chasing. It isn't something I'm comfortable doing. I always thought – '

Mercy's lips were as delicately shaped as rose petals. Mace feared he might crush them with the touch of his own lips. However, they were warm, sweet, and yielding. Even as he engulfed her in his arms, he couldn't believe such a desirable woman would want him. Holding her close, their lips entwined -- an intoxicating fantasy, a wondrous dream come true. He was so enraptured by the embrace he didn't feel her hands against his chest until she forcibly pulled away.

'Gracious!' she exclaimed. 'Don't you believe in allowing a girl to catch her breath?' She put her hand to her hair, fiddling with the curls as if her coiffure had been mussed. 'Anyone would think you never kissed a girl before.'

'Never one as sweet as you, Mercy,' he freely admitted. 'I kind of got carried away.'

'You acted as if you wanted to carry me away with you,' she joked.

He offered a sly simper. 'That's not a bad idea.'

Mercy was serious again. 'It is until your sharecroppers can live in peace. Su Lee and Liu Yung deserve a chance for happiness – the same as you and I.'

'I'll do what I can, Mercy. I'm glad you're family is with us instead of against us.'

'I was a little afraid of the Chinese at first. I mean, they have unusual customs and dress, but they were always very polite and well behaved. Once I met Su Lee, I never had any doubts about them again.'

'I felt much the same way. It's why everyone coming to this country should learn the language. Nothing worse than not being able to talk out a problem or discuss things rationally.'

'Has Wilcox sent for the U.S. Marshal? He might be able to help control Havelock.'

'It would take weeks to get anyone here. If you recall, I did that job for a living. There are way too few lawmen to cover the amount of country. Judge Morrison was only available because he was on the western swing of his circuit when my case came up. He isn't do back for another couple months.'

'You've an odd way of saying you are in this alone.'

'There's Tincup – '

'An old man, who hardly measures up against any gunman around.'

'And the sheriff – '

'I think Tincup is more competent in a fight,' she countered again.

'And there's your brother.'

She scoffed. 'Rodney is in love with Lori Havelock. He hardly counts.'

Mace skewed his expression. 'Rodney has a hankering for Seth's wife?'

She shrugged. 'He had to tell someone. Not being Catholic, we don't confide our darkest secrets to a priest – we tell each other our woes.' At Mace's frown, she hurried to add. 'Not that Rodney has ever acted on his feelings. He and Lori have only spoken a few times, but he used to see her when he would hang around with Whitey and Renz.' She uttered an unladylike grunt. 'He's a total mess.'

'He seems like a fighter, though.'

She laughed at the notion. 'You beat him with a single punch. And I can out-shoot him. The truth is, until I decided I'd rather be a lady than a tomboy, I could whip him at wrestling. Don't count on him for much help, because I don't want him getting killed.'

Mace said, 'You didn't have to eliminate all of my help. This fight sounded better when there were four of us.'

'You can count on me! I can shoot.'

'I won't risk involving you, not unless Havelock has someone attack your ranch a second time.'

'What I'm telling you, Mace, is not to count on anyone but yourself. I'm sure Wilcox, Tincup and Rodney will do what they can, but you are going to have to carry the bulk of the load.'

'I think maybe I should get my horse and just ride out,' he said.

Mercy rose up to her toes and kissed him lightly on the lips. 'Well,' she said, displaying a coquettish wink. 'You do what you think is best.'

He reached for her, but she ducked under his grasp. The move was so adroit, he figured she was likely telling the truth about being able to best Rodney in a wrestling match.

'I think we better go inside,' she said. 'I bought one of the fancy imported nightgowns for Su Lee. I want to see her face when she opens the present.'

'You'll embarrass her to tears,' he warned her.

'She'll love it,' Mercy argued. 'Not as much as her new husband, but she'll love it.'

'What a romantic you are.'

Flashing a mischievous simper, 'I want one just like it for my wedding night.'

Mace didn't get a chance to comment on that, being pulled into the crowded room. He had to be content to watch a joyous Su Lee opening a small pile of useful gifts. With them just starting out, they needed most everything.

Watching the young couple, Mace changed his last thought. In truth, people didn't need material goods or wealth; having the right person in your life was paramount. Su Lee and her new husband had the ingredient needed most – love, and each other.

The celebration lasted until well after dark. Mace stayed after everyone else was gone, seeking a moment with Su. The company had bought them a bed and a few necessities, but Mace had been preoccupied and not bought a gift. Instead, when he shook Liu's hand, he left in it a twenty-dollar bill.

Su had been the perfect hostess, seeing each guest to the door. At last. She came and took hold of Mace's arm, walking with him as if they were the dearest of friends. Before opening the door, she managed a bright smile.

'I will never forget you helped make my marriage to Liu Yung possible, Mr Banyon.'

'The pleasure was all mine. Having seen you together, any other union would have been the wrong one.'

'Perhaps you will do as well,' she said slyly. 'I wonder how long before I am invited to *your* wedding.' At his surprised look, she added: 'Even a blind man would see there is something special between you and Miss Paxton.'

Mace gulped down his embarrassment. 'Well, we've got some problems to be solved first.'

'As for us, we will do a fine job for the Temple company. We will earn the deed to our property by making him a lot of money.'

'I'm sure you two will do just fine.'

She opened the door and he stepped outside. He looked back at her and said: 'I'll miss having you as my housekeeper and cook. Liu is a lucky man.'

'It is my place now, being here with him.'

'I agree. No man likes to face the world alone. A good woman makes life worthwhile, and you will make Liu's life rich and full.'

'Thank you, Mr Banyon, and remember those words, for it works both ways. A woman – even one as beautiful as Mercy Paxton – needs a good man to love and share her life with.'

He didn't have to reply. Her statement said it all.

Chapter Thirteen

Mercy spoke causally to Su, but she could tell the girl was uncomfortable riding alongside her in the Paxton wagon. It had surprised her when Su agreed to go into town with her. Su needed several things for her new household, and thanks to Mace's wedding gift, she had the money to get most of what was needed.

'It's going to take some getting used to,' Su admitted after a time, 'not being able to walk to the center of town in a matter of minutes. Working at the main house, I never had to plan very far ahead. Now I must try and prepare a week in advance.'

'You're welcome to go into town with me to shop, Su. I hate to make the long trip alone.'

Su smiled. 'You are a very nice person.'

'I think the same about you,' Mercy replied, and the both laughed.

After a moment or two, Su grew serious.

'I fear for Mr Banyon's life, Mercy. Mr Havelock can be very ruthless, and his men are cruel and dangerous.'

'They are a worthless bunch,' Mercy agreed, 'but Mace is a very capable man. He was a deputy marshal for a number of years, so he knows how to deal with men like Havelock.'

'I know he likes you very much,' Su said boldly. 'I think you like him too.'

Mercy looked at the road ahead, as a warmth crept up from her throat and infused her cheeks with color. 'I do like him, although we haven't spent much time together.'

'He has honor and cares about other people and justice. Those are fine qualities in any man.'

Mercy could agree with that, but it was in Mace's arms that she had lost her senses. She was drawn to his touch, his lips, the inner strength she perceived in him. There was no one reason she could fathom, but she knew he was the only man in the world for her.

The town was alive and stirring, with many people on the street. Tong was between the Chinese part of town and Kemph's store, evidently shopping for some supplies for the Banyon house. Mercy waved at Rodney, who was following the old man from a few steps away. He was present to head off any trouble before it started – or so he hoped. He hurried his step, getting to the front of the store in time to lend a hand down from the buckboard to Su Lee Yung and Mercy.

He greeted them both, but remained out on the walk, keeping watch from a distance again.

***

Havelock watched the goings-on from across the street. He chewed furiously on his cigar, trying to formulate a new plan of action. He would have control of the valley by now – if it hadn't been for Banyon's interference. He ought to turn Renz loose – let him call Banyon out and kill him. Even as he thought of it, he dismissed the idea. Judge Morrison had given him a stern warning the last time Vinny Renz had gotten into trouble. If Renz killed Banyon, he would have to send him away, hundreds of miles out of the country. Without Whitey Curn, it left only Bruno to back him. He would lack the leverage and strength to finish running the Chinese out of the valley. It was a rotten situation.

Seth clamped down on his cigar, a raw hatred filling his chest. Lori had started up the street to come to work, and veered over to say good morning to Rodney. It didn't take a Pinkerton Eye to guess she was spilling her guts to the Paxton mongrel.

She would sell Seth, his bank, and every man on his payroll down the river the first chance she got. Even as he watched, she broke into a warm smile of greeting for Rodney. He pounded his fist into the open palm of his other hand. She never smiled at *him* in such a way!

Bruno, who had been keeping an eye on Banyon, came lumbering along the street. Havelock opened the door, caught the big man's attention, and drew a line across his throat. As Bruno wrinkled his forehead to question the action, Seth pointed to Rodney and his wife. The big brute looked over at them and nodded his understanding. Hitching up his belt, he shook the muscles loose in his massive shoulders and headed that way.

Seth lit his cigar and waited for the fun to begin. Bruno wouldn't have returned to the main part of town unless Banyon was occupied for a period of time. He snickered wickedly. 'Let's see how you like watching your secret boyfriend get torn limb from limb, my dear, would-be-adulterous wife!'

Bruno approached Rodney and Lori, visibly thinking of the best way to start a fight. His head snapped back when Tong came out of Kemph's store. It was the incentive he was looking for.

'What do you think you're doing, slant eyes?' he bellowed, moving to block Tong's path. 'This store ain't for you Chinese. You have your own store in the Chinaman district.'

'I go home,' Tong said, attempting to go around Bruno.

But the big man gave him a shove and knocked the grocery bag out of his arms. Bruno followed it up by pushing him a second time -- hard enough that he fell down.

'You should have stayed home – back in China!'

Rodney knew he was facing trouble. Pushing Lori gently out of the way, he helped Tong to his feet. Then he turned to face Bruno.

'Let him be, Bruno,' Rodney pleaded. 'You and the others put the Chinese store out of business for a few days. This is the only place they can shop until it's back in operation.'

'I think they can starve a little!' Bruno blasted Rodney. 'They don't care if the rest of the farmers in the valley starve – why should we care if they do too?'

Tong quietly picked up the items on the ground and put them back in his sack. However, when he stood up again, Bruno reached out and swatted it out of his hands a second time. This time, he didn't let the man bend over to pick up the goods. He grabbed him bodily and threw him against the side of the building.

Rodney yelled at him to stop, but Bruno hit Tong full in the face, driving him solidly against the wall a second time. As the old man collapsed, Rodney grabbed one of Bruno's arms to stop him.

Bruno turned on him, launching a blow to Rodney's head with a meaty fist. It knocked him off of his feet. Before he could recover, Bruno attacked him. Lori screamed for someone to help, to stop the savage onslaught, but no one was about to interfere.

Rodney pulled his elbows in tight and used his hands to try and protect himself, but Bruno hammered him several times.

Tong got to his feet, but did not run. Rodney had been helping him and he could not leave him to face the bully alone. He grabbed Bruno's arms from behind, but the huge man was much too strong. It was like trying to tackle a full-sized bull. Bruno tossed him aside like a rag doll.

Rodney regained his feet and reached for his gun. Bruno was too quick, slapping the young man's arms downward, then wrapping him up in a torturous bear hug. As Rodney struggled in his grasp, the big man began to crush him to his chest, driving the air from his lungs, forcing him to cry out from the pressure. It was only seconds before Bruno broke his back.

Tong knew he couldn't do anything barehanded, so he grabbed a tool from the rack at the front of the store. He recalled Mace had used a pick handle to beat Bruno once before. This item still had the striker attached. Thinking only of saving Rodney's life, he lifted the tool in the air and slammed the hammer down on the back of Bruno's skull!

Bruno released his hold at once, His arms went limp as he sank straight down onto the ground. Rodney collapsed with him, seeking to suck air into his lungs. It took him several breaths before he recovered enough strength to get to his feet.

Lori, Tong and Rodney stared at the lifeless form on the ground. Bruno's eyes were wide open, as was his mouth, the shock of dying the last expression he would ever make. Tong had killed him.

***

Banyon paced the sheriff's office, stopping once more to look at the angry crowd that had gathered. They were in an ugly mood, and hadn't yet started drinking.

'What'll we do, Banyon?' Wilcox wanted to know. 'I've never had to face a lynch mob before, and I can tell you I don't want to start now.'

Mace looked around at the feeble walls of the wooden structure. The thin boards wouldn't stop bullets, and there was not even a back way out. The single cell wasn't built to keep people out, only in, so it would be of little protection for Tong.

Mercy had taken her brother home to recuperate, so that left only the three of them to contend with the entire town. Tincup was keeping an eye on Renz from a discreet distance, so he and Wilcox were guarding the jail.

'It's a clear case of self-defense,' Mace said. 'If Tong hadn't stopped Bruno, he'd have killed Rodney Paxton.'

'I know that,' the sheriff replied, 'but being innocent isn't going to help us stop a mob. Renz and Havelock have been firing them up most of the day. Come nightfall, and with the aid of some free whiskey, those men will come to hang him – whether you and I are here or not.'

'We'll have to divert the mob before it gets here.'

'And how do we do that, Banyon? Are you going to simply step out and tell them they can't have him?'

'That probably wouldn't work. Renz will be ready to take us on this time – scatter-guns or not.'

'So what can we do?'

Wilcox was scared. He had accepted the job of sheriff for the added income, and outside of picking up a drunk who got a little boisterous, he had coasted along in the position. Now that he was faced with a life-or-death situation, he wanted no part of it.

'We'll move him to the county seat. Even Morrison would agree that a change of location is called for in this instance.'

The sheriff pointed at the group in the street. 'Take a look again, Banyon. Do you think those people are going to let us take Tong out, put him on a horse, and simply ride out of town?'

'As soon as it gets dark, Tincup will be reporting in. I've got an idea that might work.'

'All right,' Wilcox didn't ask his idea. 'If it works, then what?'

''Then, if the crowd gets too rowdy, you and Tincup can leave.'

'Leave?' He scowled. 'You mean leave you and Tong to face a lynch mob?'

Banyon showed a silly simper. 'Trust me, Sheriff. If we live that long, we've got a chance of seeing another day.'

Wilcox stood at the door, a shotgun in his hands. Soon as Mace was outside, he bolted the door. Most of the people glared at Mace, and a few made snide remarks or catcalls, but they didn't have the false courage liquor provided. None of them were yet willing to test Mace's resolve – let alone, his deadly accuracy with a gun.

Mace kept a wary eye to make sure he wasn't followed, but the crowd lost interest in him as soon as he was out of sight. At the moment, they were more interested in the man in the cell, rallying their numbers and nerve to attempt and take the prisoner by force.

Mace reached his house, but didn't light a lamp. He remained deep in the shadows and kept watch out the window, in case Havelock had a plan to be rid of him. There was no sign of anyone following and everything looked pretty normal.

'Mr Banyon?' a voice asked quietly. He whirled about, drew with blinding speed, and trained his gun on the darkest corner of the room.

'Wait!' Lori cried, moving out where he could see her. 'It's me!'

'Whew!' he said. 'You about gave me heart failure.'

'You?' she flared back at him. 'I'm the one who about got a bullet through my chest.'

Mace's eyes were more accustomed to the dark of the room now. He took a step closer and saw Lori's face. She had a bruise on one cheek and a black eye that was nearly swollen shut.

'What happened to you, Mrs Havelock?'

She stood erect, straightening her back. 'I hate that name. Won't you please call me Lori?'

'If you like.'

'Seth was quite put out that things didn't work out for him today. With Bruno and Whitey both gone, he has to rely on Renz. The odds are dwindling, and he doesn't like that. Bruno was supposed to kill Rodney ... and he was quite unhappy things didn't work out that way. On the whole, he had a bad day ... and took it out on me.'

'Why come to me? I'm not a lawman.'

'I want to get away from him, Mr Banyon. I am willing to do anything to escape.' She ducked her head as she spoke. 'I have been a dutiful wife but I can no longer endure being close to such a cold-hearted beast. He has threatened me many times, but he never raised his hand before.' Her voice grew stronger. 'I warned him when we said our vows that I would not tolerate abuse. The Good Book says a woman can leave a husband if he beats her. Well, he beat me, and I'm leaving!'

'I'm surprised he didn't get rough with you when you testified in court to save my hide.'

'That's why I came to you ... Mace Banyon. I think you owe me a favor.'

Banyon swallowed hard. He did owe her a favor, and he did not like being in debt. 'What do you want of me, Lori?'

'I've got a little money. Not much, but enough to get by until I can find work and a place to stay. If you can get me to the train station, or even some place where I can take a stage for Santa Fe or Albuquerque ... any place where I can start over.'

'You know Rodney is in love with you.'

She bit her lower lip. 'I ... I have feelings for Rodney too, but I can't put him in danger.'

'Tell you what,' he said. 'I'll take you to the Paxton farm. This battle is coming to a head, and I intend to put an end to Seth's tyranny. If things work out, you might not have to worry about him any longer. Once in jail, it's much easier to get a proper divorce.'

'Whatever you think, Mr Banyon. My only goal is to get away from him.'

'I'm going out back and will saddle three horses – you can ride, can't you?' At her nod, he went on with the plan. 'Look through what we have in the cupboards and put together enough supplies for two people for a couple days. If things work out, I'll be back in about an hour. I'll see you as far as the Paxton farm on my way out of town.'

'Whatever you say, Mr Banyon.'

Mace didn't speak again, turning for the back of the house. What could he say? He couldn't tell Lori that everything would turn out all right, for there were too many uncertainties. He had no evidence against Havelock, no way to prove that Seth was mixed up in the mob action. He couldn't even prove him guilty of turning loose Bruno on Rodney. Even with Lori's testimony – and wives could not testify against their husbands – the man had kept himself out of the picture. To a court of law, he was as innocent as any bystander.'

Banyon closed the back door behind him, then stopped to look around. It was early dusk, and the shadows were long and dark, so he took care to search the place before exposing himself to a sniper's bullet. Moments passed and there was no one lurking near with a gun. He told himself to be quiet, cool, and calculating. It would take all of his skill to get Tong out of town. Even then, that might only be the beginning of his troubles.

Chapter Fourteen

Carrying an innocent looking picnic basket, Mace returned to the jail as darkness covered the town. Tincup was already there waiting for him.

'Wilcox said you had a plan?'

Mace opened the basket. 'Have Tong put these clothes on.'

'Hey! Them's my clothes!'

'Tong's about the same size as you. I'll need your hat too.'

Tincup understood what he had in mind, and Wilcox moved over to stand guard at the window, making sure no one was able to see inside the jail.

Tong complained about the tightness and restriction of such clothes, and he didn't like wearing boots or Tincup's floppy old hat, but they finally got him dressed.

'It's quiet outside,' Wilcox said. 'Most of the men are getting liquored up at the saloon. 'I expect we have maybe an hour before the storm hits.'

Mace gave a nod. 'Should be ample time.'

Tincup reset the hat on Tong's head and stepped back to appraise their handiwork. 'If I didn't know better, I'd believe old Tong was me.'

'Let's hope the rest of the men who see us are no sharper than you,' Mace teased.

'Ride hard and fast, Banyon,' Wilcox told him. 'And, incidentally, take the badge I put on the desktop. If you're going to act as my deputy, you should at least have a star pinned on. It will make what you're doing legal.'

Banyon picked up the piece of tin, oddly enjoying the feel of the familiar object. He stuck it in his shirt pocket and stood at the door.

'Ready, Tong?'

'How long I wear ... Mr Kelly clothes? I no like.'

'Just till we get to the house. You can change while I get the horses loaded to ride.'

The old man shook his head. 'Me no see how men work in such clothing. It like being bound up with rope.'

'You mess up our exit out of town,' Mace warned, 'and we'll both know how it feels to be bound up with rope. Hanged too!'

Tong went out the door with Mace, and fell in on the side closest to the buildings. Anyone watching would see Mace first and only a glimpse or two of the counterfeit Tincup Kelly. Taking their time, no one approached or confronted them. They walked unmolested out of town and back to the main house.

Lori had the horses ready, including food for a meal or two. Tong quickly changed his clothes and the three of them rode off toward the Paxton farm. For better or worse, the plan was proceeding. Only time would tell if Mace had made the smart move.

***

Renz opened the door to Havelock's house, slammed it behind him, and strode angrily into the living room. Seth, who had been toying with a plate of leftover stew, looked up from the table.

'You find her?'

'She's not in town, boss. And what's worse, neither is Tong!'

'What?' Havelock came up out of his chair. 'Where is Tong?'

Renz swore. 'Banyon sneaked him out of town. No one knows how he did it. I stirred up some men and we stormed the jail, only to find out Wilcox had left the door open. We got inside and no one was there, not Tong, not Wilcox ... nobody!'

Seth forgot his hunger. He paced around the room, enraged at being played a fool by both Lori and Banyon.

'What does that man think he can do, play with us like a cat with a couple of mice?'

'You should have let me kill him.'

Seth said: 'A little late for that now. Who do you know in Pine City?'

Renz frowned. 'You think that's where he's headed?'

'Of course. It's the county seat. The sheriff over there has three deputies, and he's a tough man to deal with. Wilcox and Banyon would certainly try and get Tong over there for trial.'

Renz thought for a moment. 'The Xanthor brothers are over in Pine City. I've worked with them a time or two.'

'Yes, I remember a little about them. Can they be trusted?'

'For the right price, they'd turn their own mother over to a lynch mob – then put the rope around her neck themselves. Money is all they are loyal too.'

'Send a wire to them. Promise whatever amount you think it'll take to persuade them, and have them kill Banyon and Tong before they reach Pine City.'

Renz's face darkened. 'I wanted to kill that jasper myself, Seth. Whitey was a friend.'

'It can't be helped. If they find sanctuary with that sheriff, we won't have any leverage at all. We could end up being investigated for Ti Fat's murder and the vandalism of the farms around the valley.'

'OK. What about your wife?'

'To hell with her! If she went with them, the Xanthors can do whatever they please with her!'

'Damn, boss!' Renz complained. 'Wish you'd have given her to me. That little hellcat has treated me like the plague ever since you married her.'

Seth stuck on point. 'If we find her hiding out somewhere, she is all yours.' Then he added, 'Just make sure she never shows her face in this town again.'

Renz whirled about and went into the night, heading for the telegraph office. It was a full day's ride to Pine City, so he should have plenty of time to contact the Xanthor brothers.

Seth stared with disgust at the stew on his plate. He should have known better than to actually marry a woman. They were deceitful, thankless and unfaithful. He knew Lori had never cheated with her body, but her heart and mind were never his. He would have been much better off to buy himself a consort, one he could keep as long as he wanted, then discard her for another. *Like an old gun for a newer model*, he mused.

He had other things to worry about at the moment. It cost money to keep men like Whitey, Bruno and Renz on his payroll. Plus, he had a Mexican family named Gonzales to tend to his land and maintain his house. He wondered if Mrs Gonzales could prepare anything but Mexican food. He was going to need someone to cook and clean until he replaced Lori.

Considering his goal, gaining control of the Temple holdings, there were a few clouds in the sky earlier in the day. If it happened to rain, he might lose the opportunity he had waited for all these months. Everything had been within reach, before Mace Banyon arrived in the valley. Now everything was crumbling around him. If Tincup and Wilcox were laughing at him, it would be their last laugh. Renz and the Xanthors would put an end to Banyon and Tong. Then he would deal with those two and take what he wanted. A crooked smile came to his lips. He would have the last laugh!

***

Mace slowed his sorrel. It was amazing the animal had enough pep left to side-step, but the little horse was tough and sturdy. It took only a nudge of his rider's heels and he would run himself until he dropped.

'See something?' Tong asked.

'It's a feeling,' Tong,' Mace said. 'I used to get it when I was closing in on a fugitive and was expecting an ambush at any second.'

'Mr Renz could not be ahead of us.'

'No, he couldn't,' Mace agreed.

They had left Oasis undetected and ridden all night. With such a head start, Renz couldn't have caught up. There was –

Mace saw his horse's ears perk forward. Something was there!

'Duck! He shouted, reaching out to push Tong out of his saddle. It was none too soon – two gun blasts filled the early-morning air.

Mace felt the breeze of a bullet go past his head, as he rolled out of his saddle. He pulled his gun, at the same time as he landed on his knees. Behind the skittish and dancing horses, he sought to find a target. A muzzle flashed, the roar of the weapon echoing through the air once more. Instantly, Mace returned fire – a round to the exact spot of the flash and then a quick bullet to either side.

Tong started to rise, but couldn't. He'd been hit. Mace hollered at him to stay down, and darted for cover, rolling behind a mount of earth, firing rapidly into the brush.

He curled his body behind the small hill of dirt and quickly reloaded. Tong was lying flat on the ground. Mace couldn't tell if he was staying hidden or if he was wounded or dead.

Ready to fire again, Mace didn't look over the mound, but removed his hat and peeked around its edge. He could hear only his own breathing and see nothing stirring.

If the men who ambushed him were moving, they were very good at their job. Logically, they would be trying to get into a better position to kill him.

Scooting away, still flat on his stomach, Mace quickly rolled off the edge of the trail. Hearing nothing, he slithered like a snake into the foliage and continued a short way into deep cover.

He stopped then, perspiring heavily from the heat and strain. His heart sounded like a hammer on an anvil, smacking it at a terrific rate of speed. He held his breath and listened, concentrating with every bit of sensory perception he had. It sounded like –

A shadow loomed up from out of nowhere, a bearded man with a big pair of Colts, no more than fifteen feet away! Mace rolled onto his side, raising his gun – just as the man spotted him. Time ceased to flow – alarm sprang into the man's eyes, and panic rushed to his face. He tried to swing his guns round on his prey --

Mace got off the first shot – a return blast filled is ears and kicked dust into his face from one of the man's guns. Mace pulled the trigger twice more, then blinked to clear his vision. The man was not in sight.

Rubbing the dirt from his eyes, Mace listened. A haggard rasp of a man reached his ears. It was the sound of someone who had been shot through his lungs. The shooter didn't call out for help, and that caused Mace to wonder about his partner. From the opening volley, it had sounded like two rifles. The man struggling for air had brandished two Colts, but could not have fired two rifles at the same time.

Going with his natural instinct, Mace rose slowly to his feet, gun ready, searching the area for any movement.

Nothing.

He weaved his way out of the brush and spotted the bearded man on the ground. There was a pool of blood near his chest and he had both hands on the wound. His guns were in reach, but he made no effort to grab one of them.

'Looks like you're hit pretty hard,' Mace told the man quietly. 'Let me have a look. There might be something I can do.'

The man rolled his head to the side and glowered at Mace. From the ashen complexion and a sunken chest wound, he didn't have long.

'Yuh kilt my brother,' he gasped. 'Kilt him without being able to see him!'

'A lucky shot for me,' Mace admitted. 'Not so lucky for him.'

His teeth were set to control crying out from the pain, so his words hissed between them as he spoke. 'Som'thin tol me not to try and take yuh, Banyon. We pulled a couple jobs back in Kansas a year or so back – we'd heard about yuh.'

'So why did you try and kill me?'

The twisted face lit up slightly, a forced smile curling his lips. 'Fer the money – what else?'

'Who was paying you?'

'Hell, Banyon,' he grunted, then coughed from the effort, 'yuh know Havelock is the only man in the country who could afford to hire us.'

'You're the Xanthor brothers.'

Another partial sneer that could be interpreted as a smile. 'Heard 'o us too, huh?'

'I reckon most everyone in these parts knows about the Xanthors. Tough men to kill.'

The man wheezed and swallowed hard, nearly out of breath and strength. 'Not ... not tough enough. '

His eyes stared blankly into space, unseeing, and a final sigh slipped between his lips. The Xanthor brothers would kill no more.

Mace checked on Tong, but the old man had been drilled through the heart. The bushwhackers had done half of their job. He left him for a few minutes, while he located the other Xanthor. Then he scouted around and located their horses.

Being a few miles out of Pine City, Mace loaded the bodies over the horses and secured them in place. He covered each with a blanket and led the parade of dead men to town.

The greeting was a strange one. People stopped on the streets and stared, children questioned their parents as to what was going on, and two lawmen were on the step of the sheriff's office by the time he reached the jail.

A groan escaped Mace's lips when he spotted a familiar face. Judge Morrison was in town! He joined the sheriff and deputy as Mace brought his cavalcade to a halt.

'At it again, are you, Banyon?' he asked disdainfully. 'Not enough killing going on in Oasis, so you came here to continue ridding the earth of unsavory characters and undesirables?'

'I was bringing my Chinese friend over here for his protection. The two bearded gents ambushed us about three miles out of town. They didn't give me the option of arresting them.' He lifted the badge from his shirt pocket. 'This was an official act, sanctioned by Sheriff Wilcox.'

The deputy lifted the blankets to check the identities. 'Man oh man!' he exclaimed. 'This here fella did us a real service, Sheriff. It's the Xanthors!'

Mace explained his mission and how Tong had saved young Paxton's life. He finished with, 'Havelock was riling the crowd into a lynch mob, so I brought him here until a hearing could be arranged.'

The judge looked at one of the bystanders. 'Stevens?' he directed his attention to a short man with a weasel face. 'What do you know about this? And,' he added before the fellow could think up a lie, 'I will check with the telegrapher in Oasis, so you best tell the truth.'

He lowered his head. 'Uh, telegrams are confidential, Judge.'

'Tell me what you know, or I'll have you tossed in jail for contempt of court!'

The man swallowed his courage. 'I only copied the message, Judge. If I was to run to the law every time something unsavory came across my desk – ' He had to swallow a second time. 'I wouldn't live very long.'

'Tell me about the message for the Xanthors.'

'Seth Havelock offered to pay them five hundred dollars to see that Banyon and the Chinese man didn't reach Pine City. It was signed by his head man, Vinny Renz.'

Before anyone could react, Stevens lamented: 'Judge, you gotta protect me. If Renz finds out I told, he'll skin me alive ... then hurt me some more!'

The judge regarded Mace with a mixed expression, somewhere between contempt and admiration. 'Looks like you have your case against Havelock, Deputy Banyon. Conspiracy to commit murder.'

'I'd appreciate a couple warrants, Judge,' Mace said.

'Dead or alive?' he asked, his gaze narrowing.

'Alive if I can, but Renz will be tough to take – either way.'

'I'll draw up a couple,' he agreed. Then he turned to the sheriff. 'Get these bodies down to the undertaker's place.' With a look at Mace, 'unless you want to take the Oriental gentleman home with you.'

'I've been up since yesterday morning, and my horse is beat. We need a few hours rest.' With a sigh, and unable to hide his emotion, he said: 'Tong would understand if we bury him here. We'll have a service for him when I get home.'

For the first time, Judge Morrison displayed a bit of compassion. 'I'm sorry for the loss of your friend.'

'I'll see to it he didn't die in vain,' Mace replied. 'Stopping a war, and saving the lives of all the Chinese farmers – it's a noble death. Tong would be satisfied.'

Chapter Fifteen

Seth Havelock was putting up a 'Closed for Lunch' sign in the bank window when Renz opened the door. The banker could see he was not happy about something.

'OK, give me the bad news,' he said.

Renz held out a piece of paper.

'What's this?'

'A telegram from Pine City.'

Seth read the message and looked at his hired man. 'The Xanthors are dead, and there are warrants out for our arrest?' He felt an inner scream of frustration, mixed with a dreaded apprehension. 'How could that be?' he asked. 'What warrants could they have? We've done nothing to give ourselves away.'

'Who knows? Maybe Lori shot off her mouth. With you two on the outs, there might be some way for her to testify against you.'

Seth discarded the notion. 'A woman can't legally testify against her husband. It must be something else.'

'Well, the Xanthors aren't going to get on the witness stand and testify against us, boss.'

'Maybe Su Lee and Mercy saw me give Bruno the signal to kill Rodney.'

Renz was incredulous. 'You did that, right out in the open?'

'I lost my head for a moment,' Havelock excused his lack of judgment. 'Lori was cozying up to Rodney and I didn't think straight. I motioned to Bruno – ' he ran his finger across his throat -- 'like this. Any jury in the country would interpret that to mean I wanted Rodney killed.'

'And those two gals witnessed it?'

'Not that I saw at the time, but I was looking at Bruno. I have no idea if either of them were looking my way.'

'But how does that implicate me?' Renz wondered. 'The warrants are for us both.'

Seth tried to reason it out. 'Lori *could* testify against you. I'm protected from anything she saw or knows, but you aren't. Remember, she was in the next room when you and Whitey showed up with Ti Fat. Even though Bruno and Whitey did the actually killing, you were a part of it.'

Renz groaned. 'We're getting in a deep hole here, boss. 'Maybe we ought to take what money we can and get out of the country.'

'We still have one chance left.'

'Yeah, the chance we take when we make a run for the tall cedar and open spaces. I don't know about you, but I can't outrun a bullet!'

'There's another way,' Seth said.

Renz didn't like the way this was shaping up, but he waited to hear Havelock's plan.

'An act of reprisal is in order against the Chinese. I suggest a fire tonight, while Su Lee and her new husband are asleep.'

'Holy Hannah! You want – '

Seth lifted a hand to stop his protest. 'The Chinese will be angered and want revenge. They will kill the Paxtons, and there are no witnesses against us.'

Renz was in awe. 'Boss, you're the most cold-blooded man I ever met.'

'I left the war with little more than the shirt on my back. I started my first bank in Texas with only a couple hundred dollars. I haven't worked and sweated blood to get this far just to see it all flutter away in the wind. If you haven't got the stomach for it – '

'I can handle my end,' Renz told him coldly. 'But what about Lori?'

'I overheard Wilcox's wife buying some extra groceries ... for the Paxton family.' Renz's blank look said he hadn't a clue what that meant. 'Lori is there!' he told him patiently. 'The only other place she could take refuge is at Banyon's place, but Tincup was here with Wilcox, and Banyon and the Chinese were on their way to Pine City. Lori wouldn't stay alone; she must be at the Paxton place.'

'It makes sense. I haven't seen Rodney since all of this took place.'

'Because he's busy being a hero for my wife. The two of them are probably planning their wedding, as soon as I'm in jail or dead.'

'All right, but where is the payoff?' Renz wanted to know. 'I mean, even if all of this works out, we still have Banyon to deal with and Temple still has all of his farmers.'

'If we make sure he loses his crops this season, it will make the valley a bad investment. He'll sell, and he'll sell cheap. When he does, I'll make you a full partner – fifty percent of everything I own.'

'So how do I make it look like the Chinese attacked the Paxton place. I mean, we're talking killing all four people – plus one more if your wife is there.'

'You'll have to tie them up. Use a light-weight rope that will burn off in the fire.'

'Damn,' Renz breathed. 'This is a lot for one man to do.'

'You burn down the Chinese shack tonight and I'll help you with the Paxtons afterward. If Lori is there, I want to give her a little special treatment.'

'Banyon will be back tomorrow. That doesn't leave us but tonight, boss.'

'We hit one early and the other a couple hours after that.'

'That's expecting everything to go right. But what if Tincup and Wilcox show up? They are going to be doing something while all this is going on.'

'If they get in the way, we'll have to deal with them,' Havelock said. 'This is it for us, Renz. We either get this done right, or we pack and run.'

A sneer came to his lips. 'I've never run from nobody or nothing. I just hope I get a chance at Banyon before this is all over.'

'You can count on that, my friend. Banyon won't believe for a minute that his coolies would resort to violence. He'll come looking for us.'

'I think he's sweet on Mercy Paxton too,' Renz said. 'It will be nice to not have to worry about him again. The man has been a menace since the day he arrived.'

'You're certain you can take him?'

Renz laughed. 'If he drew square against Whitey – and your wife said he did – and Whitey got off a shot at the same time as him, it means the two of them were about equal with a gun. I could have taken Whitey a hundred times out of a hundred tries.'

'All right.' Seth was satisfied. 'Better tell Axle to be ready to help with our alibis tonight and then get some rest. It's going to be a long night.'

***

Mace awoke from his slumber. He pulled his pocket watch from his trousers and looked at it. He had been asleep for almost six hours ... long enough.

He was driven by a sense of urgency to get back to Oasis. He didn't relish facing Su Lee and the other Chinese people, to inform them of the loss of one of their long-time leaders. He patted the warrants in his shirt pocket and the deputy sheriff's badge was pinned on his vest. If he could bring the culprits to justice, the Chinese would be satisfied. If not –'

I'll be dead, so I will have done the best I could do!

Strapping on his gun, he glanced at the haggard face that peered back from the cracked mirror on the wall. He didn't waste time shaving. Every minute counted.

It was darker than usual for that time of day and, gazing skyward, Mace saw the reason why. There were massive, rolling clouds covering the dying sun. The drought was about over.

What would Seth Havelock do now?

With his horse carrying him on short rest, he kept up a steady pace. Topping the ridge where he had fought the Xanthor brothers, he stopped his horse for a breather. At the same time, he donned his rain slicker. Several drops were splatting in the dust and striking his shirt, hat and vest. The ground was still dry, and he determined he was at the front of the storm. It was following him, but the clouds were moving faster than he could travel. He would soon be riding in both the rain and the dark. It would slow him down considerably. He had hoped to make Oasis before midnight. With the rain, it would put it closer to daylight.

'Let's go, boy!' he said to his horse. The little sorrel responded, taking off in an easy lope.

Chapter Sixteen

Tincup remained hidden in the depths of the shadows, watching with a fascinated curiosity. Renz had a container of coal oil strapped to the side of his horse. Renz had been holed up in his room most of the afternoon, so whatever he had planned, it either took a great deal of consideration, or needed the cover of night. Staying in the dark, he watched Renz ride quietly past. Then he set out to get his own horse.

There was a gusting wind, and the smell of rain was in the air, even though they hadn't gotten a drop of moisture as yet. Tincup followed a hundred yards behind the gunman, worried about his plan. Rain wouldn't help stave off a war if Havelock's hired gun started killing people.

They followed a trail along the river for a time, before Renz cut across country. It was wide open land, and Tincup could hardly make him out against the blackness of the stormy night. He wished some of the far-flung lightning would strike closer so he could see better. Just then, heaven answered with a distant flash and he stopped his horse. Renz was gone!

Tincup pulled his gun and listened. Sitting in the dark was like being enclosed in a closet with the door closed. It was too gloomy to see more than a few feet in any direction. He searched for landmarks, but could seen nothing but open fields. He had an idea where he was, but had never come this way from the creek. He knew the stream wound to the east and the open ground belonged to Su Lee and her new husband. In fact, their home could not be far ….

The realization hit Tincup like one of the distant lightning bolts! The cans of fuel were to start a fire, but Renz wasn't going after crops this time. He was going to burn down Su Lee's place!

Tincup turned his horse towards the young couple's dwelling. Their home was built out of old cedar and pine. It would go up like shaved tinder. There would be little time to get out if the place was torched.

Even as Tincup thought of it, a bright flash lit up the end of the valley. He drove his heels into the horse, recklessly racing across plowed fields. Every second would count.

By the time he arrived, the flames were shooting up from the side and front of the house, already engulfing the roof. The doorway was an inferno, and Renz had fired the side with the only window. Su Lee and her husband were trapped!

Tincup was not a man to panic, thinking quickly. The house had two rooms, and the window was over the kitchen counter. The bedroom was protected by an inner wall, and it was farthest from the flames. He had one chance, if he could find something to work with.

He yanked his horse to a skidding stop, then used the fire's light to search around the outside of the house. He found the ax sticking into a tree stump where Liu cut the wood for their stove. Grabbing it up, Tincup raced around to the back of the house, where he expected the young couple to be. Like a madman, he began to hack and chop at the wall. He threw all of his strength into the cutting, feeling only the urgency to make a decent-sized hole in the building.

He could hear Su Lee crying, and both she and Liu were coughing from the smoke. He increased his frenzy, chopping faster and harder. At last he kicked the last couple of boards free with his boot, then crawled into the room.

'The heavy smoke assailed Tincup's lungs and eyes. Su was on the floor covering Liu with her own body. He had tried to help Tincup from the inside, but had passed out from the heat and smoke.

'Get out!' Tincup yelled at Su. "I'll bring Liu Yung!'

Su crawled for the opening, choking for enough air to remain conscious. Tincup gave her a hard push through the hole, then grabbed hold of her husband's wrists.

The heat was unbearable, a wall of flame devouring everything in its path. With sheer determination Tincup exerted all of his remaining strength dragging Liu to the exit hole.

Su reached in and helped pull Liu out. Before Tincup could follow, the roof collapsed.

A cry, a scream that echoed into the night, was the last thing Tincup heard. Heavy timber crashed down on his head and shoulders, knocking him senseless. Even as he felt Su's hands on his wrists, he was sinking into a pit of darkness.

***

The rains came. Like a torrent beneath a waterfall, great sheets of water pelted the parched land. Streaks of lightning split the night. The bellowing roar of thunderclaps rocked the earth.

Mace ducked his head against his chest, trying to see through the dark wall of water. Had he not been on the main road, he would have been lost in minutes. The blackness and rain obscured even the most familiar landmarks, and he traveled hours along the road without an inkling of where he was.

Fortune lent a hand in that a crack of lightning happened to light the small path that led from the the main road to the Paxton house. Deciding it would be better to put up in the barn than continue fighting the rain for another three miles into town, he reined his horse in that direction.

As he entered the yard, Mace felt a cold lump form in his chest. A carriage – one he recognized as belonging to the town doctor – was parked in front of the Paxton house. Even more troubling, he saw Tincup's favorite horse tethered next to it. The lights were burning throughout the house, and someone's head appeared at the window as he rode up to the hitching post. A sentry keeping watch in the wee hours of the morning – something very bad was in the wind.

'That you, Banyon?' Rodney's voice called out.

'It's me,' Mace responded. 'What's going on?'

'Come in out of the rain. I'll tell Mercy to get you a cup of coffee.'

Mace shook off as much water as he could, removed his slicker, once under the shelter of the porch awning, and stepped into the warm front room.

Su Lee was sitting next to her husband. He had bandages around one arm and hand, and another wrapped about his head. Both them and their clothes were streaked with soot, though Su looked a little better. She only had a single bandage wrapped around one of her wrists. She gave him a reassuring smile and greeted him.

'So happy to have you back, Mr Banyon.' Then she glanced past him. 'Is Father safely in jail at Pine City?'

Mace put off the question. 'What's happened here? Where is Tincup?'

'He was watching Renz in town,' Rodney told him. 'He followed him out to Su Lee and Liu Yung's house. He arrived too late to stop him from setting fire to their place, but he managed to cut a hole in the back so they could escape.'

'And?' Mace prompted when Rodney hesitated.

'Tincup saved us,' Su put in, her voice cracking noticeably. 'He pushed me and Liu out, but the roof caved in on him. I managed to pull him out, and he mumbled who had set the fire. Those were the only words he spoke before he passed out.'

'He's still unconscious,' Mercy chipped in, having been pouring Mace a cup of coffee. She handed it to him and sighed. 'The doctor has been with him for about thirty minutes.'

Mace took a sip and enjoyed the warmth it brought to his cold, damp body. Even so, the taste was bitter – not the coffee, but the situation.

'Havelock must be desperate to try something like this,' Mercy said. 'What good would killing Su and her husband have done?'

'Might have started a war,' Mace replied. 'If I'm not mistaken,

Havelock probably knows about the warrants I have for his and Renz's arrests. If they got a full-scale war going before I got back, they could get rid of witnesses until there was no case against them.'

'I didn't know we had a case against them,' Rodney said. 'Lori can't testify against Havelock, being that she's still married to him.'

'Seth made a mistake in hiring the Xanthors to kill me and Tong ... ' Mace stopped speaking, aware of the sharp interest Su suddenly showed in his statement.

'He hired men to kill you and my father?'

The fear of what Mace had to tell her flooded her face. He swallowed his regret and related details of the ambush. He finished with, 'Tong died instantly, Su. He felt no pain.'

The girl did not gush her sorrow, no fit of tears or sobbing. Su was a strong woman. Instead, she turned away and laid her head against her husbands shoulder. He wrapped his arm about her and held her close.

'Who did you say bushwhacked you?' Rodney wanted to know. 'You called them the Xanthors?'

'Two outlaw brothers from Pine City. I was lucky – they were not.'

Mercy came across the room and, unashamed, put her arms around Mace. She ignored the wetness of his outfit as it dampened her blouse and skirt, hugging him tightly for a few short seconds. When she pushed back, she looked at him and asked: 'What are we going to do now?'

Before he could answer, Lori Havelock entered the room. Her face was drawn and pale, from fear, angst, and lack of sleep.

'Mr Banyon,' she said gently, 'Tincup is awake and is asking for you.'

Mace went forward as Mercy quickly moved to one side. He paused in front of Lori. 'How is he?'

The young lady shook her head. 'It wasn't just the roof caving in on him,' she said gently. 'The doctor thinks his heart gave out from stress and exertion.'

Mace sucked in a breath to put on a mask of cheerfulness, then entered the room. Ed Paxton and the doctor were leaving Tincup's bedside. He stopped the doctor, searching his face for a clue as to how bad it was. He didn't like either man's expression.

'Better talk to him now,' the doctor advised. 'I'm afraid Mr Kelly won't be with us much longer. I'm surprised he regained consciousness at all.'

It was devastating news, but Mace hurried to his friend's bedside without delay.

The room was dark, except for a lamp turned low in one corner. A chair was next to the bed, so Mace sat down. He examined the pallid, dirty face of the elderly man everyone called Tincup. The man's eyes were shut, but they flicked open enough to see him, then closed again from the effort.

'You made good time,' Tincup whispered hoarsely. 'I figured I'd have to hold on till morning.'

'Come morning, I'll kick your tail out of bed.' Mace instilled a forced confidence in his voice. 'I refuse to believe you can't shake off a little bump on the head – I mean, you're a genuine hero!'

Tincup's lips curled ever so slightly at the corners. 'I was hoping to back your play against Renz and Havelock.'

'You still can,' Mace offered. 'I'm going to wait until the rain stops. Probably be noon by then.'

'No, I think I need a long rest,' the weak voice argued. 'I'm tired, Banyon. And – well, what-the-hay! I don't want to sit in some rocking-chair and watch the world go by. If I can't be a part of things that make life worth living, I don't want no part of it at all.'

'You're young yet, Tincup. I need you to oversee the farms.'

Again a semblance of a smile, a wisp of humor on his lips. 'I done my share, Banyon. Now it's up to you.'

Mace put his hand out and rested it on the man's frail shoulder. 'A few hours,' he said. 'That's all I can afford for you to take. You've still got a lot ... '

But the man's mouth had gone slack and his chest showed no movement. Tincup had seen his last sunset, fought his last fight. He died a hero, saving the lives of a young married couple. Not a bad epitaph when leaving this world.

Mace didn't leave right away. He remained in the subdued light, blinking at tears that burned the backs of his eyes. He was weary from the long hours in the saddle, worn down by the heavy rain, and still soaked to the bone. It took several minutes before he inverted the grief to anger. The rising ire gave him renewed strength.

'Damn Havelock's greed and the cold-blooded attempt by Renz and Axle to kill two innocent people,' he grated to the lifeless corpse. 'I won't let them go unpunished for causing your death, Tincup. They'll either pay through the court of law and be hanged, or I'll deal out justice myself!'

Mace rose to his feet, bid Tincup a final farewell, then went out of the bedroom.

His sorrowful expression was enough to inform everyone in the room that Tincup had passed away. The grim determination showed what Mace had in mind and Rodney was quickly on his feet.

'I'm riding with you, Banyon,' he grunted through the pain of his mending ribs.

'No you're not!' Ed Paxon told him. 'You're in no shape to sit a horse. You can't even pull on your own boots yet.'

'I agree with your father,' the doctor said. 'The pain would have you folded at the middle and you might undo all of the good the support bandages are doing.'

'Mace needs someone to watch his back,' Rodney fought back.

'He can get Wilcox for that,' Ed said. 'After all, he's the sheriff of Oasis.'

'I don't need any help,' Mace told them. 'Seth and Renz have gone out of their way to make trouble for me and the whole valley. I reckon I'll give them what they want – even if it kills them!'

Mercy blocked his path to the door, her eyes misted from crying. Looking at her candid concern for his welfare, he felt his anger diminish. This was the woman he loved, and he would do anything to please her – anything, except forget about Tincup, Havelock and Renz.

'For my sake, Mace,' she murmured. 'Take Sheriff Wilcox with you. If nothing else, it will make anything you have to do legal.'

Mace didn't want Wilcox in the way, nor did he wish to let the man get himself killed during a fight. He donned his rain slicker and stepped out onto the porch. He tried to close the door, but Mercy had followed after him. She came swiftly into his arms.

He looked down at her, but was unprepared for her act of persuasion. She kissed him, pulling him so tight against her he could almost feel her heart beating.

'Promise me that you'll take Wilcox with you, Mace,' she pleaded. 'I don't want to live without you, so please do as I ask … just this one time!'

He stared at her in the dark, knowing he would never be able to deny her anything her heart desired. She wasn't asking him not to go – simply to take the sheriff along.

'All right, Mercy,' he finally agreed. 'I'll visit Wilcox first thing.'

'No.' It wasn't what she wanted to hear. 'Promise me that you will take him *with you*. I don't want you facing Renz and Havelock alone.'

He frowned. 'You're kind of hard to please.'

A mischievous simper played on Mercy's lips, her oval face illuminated by the light shining through the front window. 'I chose you, didn't I?'

'Seems like a contradiction to me.'

The smile faded. 'Promise me, Mace Banyon, or I'll go inside crying like a baby – and it will all be your fault!'

'All right, all right!' he gave in. 'I'll take Wilcox with me, if that's what it's going to take to make you happy.'

'Having you back in one piece will make me happy. See that you come back that way.'

He kissed her lightly, then strode out into the pouring rain.

Chapter Seventeen

The rain had turned to a drizzle by daylight. That's when Mace and Wilcox went looking for Renz and Havelock. Come to find out, they had spent the night at the Dry Wash Saloon. The only hired man there was the barkeep – Axle. Wilcox said he often did odd jobs for Seth.

When they reached the batwing doors, Mace removed his rain slicker and lifted his gun so it settled lightly in its holster. Wilcox took a moment and checked the loads in his 10-gauge twin-barrel shotgun. They looked inside before entering.

Renz and Havelock were sitting at a table, with a near-empty whiskey bottle and two glasses sitting next to a deck of idle playing cards. Axle was behind the bar, but both hands were visible at the moment. There was no worry of ambush now, for this was Renz's game. He had made it clear he thought himself superior to Mace when it came to prowess with a gun. He didn't need tricks to defeat Mace, and he was willing to face him man-to-man.

Even with the saloon empty for hours, the smoke lingered, and the smell of beer and spilled drinks reeked from the interior. Mace took his last breath of clean, rain-scented air and pushed the door open with his left hand.

Havelock gave him a nonchalant look. His eyes were red from drink and lack of sleep, but he would be dangerous. A cruel smile twisted a crooked line along his lips.

'Wa'al, gud' morning, Sheriff,' he drawled. 'I've been expecting you.'

'We've got warrants for your arrest, Havelock,' Mace said evenly, taking a step closer and setting himself. 'You too, Renz.'

'Been wanting to kill you for a long time,' Renz spoke up. 'If Seth had let me take care of you right after you showed up, we'd be kings of this valley. Instead, we're wanted men.'

Wilcox was next to Mace now, facing the table where Havelock was sitting. Renz had scooted his chair back and risen to his feet. His hand was inches above his gun, ready to draw and fire with a speed beyond anything Mace could match.

'You best go fetch the doc,' Wilcox told Axle. 'If this comes to gunplay, he'll be needed.'

Axle took the moment's hesitation as an out – wanting no part of a gunfight – and hurried out of the bar.

'Odds are even now, Havelock,' Mace warned. 'Why don't you both put your guns on the table and surrender to Wilcox here. Who knows? You might win your freedom in court.'

Havelock had drank a full dose of courage. With the reckless abandon hard liquor gives a man, he rose to his feet. 'You've ruined me, Banyon!' He snarled. 'You killed Whitey, the Xanthors, and were responsible for Bruno getting killed. Everything I had going in this valley, you fouled it up. I'll be damned if I give you the satisfaction of arresting me.'

'You'll be damned all right, Havelock,' Mace snapped back. 'But it's because of your actions. You and your gunnie pal caused the death of Tong Lee yesterday and my friend, Tincup Kelly last night. You're going to pay for that.'

'If it hadn't been for the rain, we would have wiped you all out!' Seth growled. 'A few more hours and you would have come back to nothing but devastation.'

'Shows that *right* was on my side ... as well as Mother Nature.'

Renz took a step back, going into a gunman's crouch. His eyes were bright, his face skewed in his desire for blood. But there had to be a glimmer of doubt – Renz had probably never faced an experienced man like Mace. The ex-marshal had been in this type of situation before.

'Being on the the right won't save you this time, Banyon!' the gunman snarled, working himself up for the contest. 'I'm gonna kill you, here and now!'

Mace already had his hand on his gun, not worried about the ethics of out-drawing a killer. He didn't have to reach, he only had to pull the gun and fire. He knew his chances were not good against a man like Renz. But he took it!

Havelock grabbed for his own pistol as Wilcox cocked back the hammers of his shotgun. Their fight would be too slow for Mace to see, as he was whipping his gun up swiftly ...

Smoke, fire and lead flashed from the muzzle of Renz's gun, the blast filling the room. Mace had rotated his body slightly with his own draw. Knowing, at best, he would get off a single shot, he made it count. He felt the sting of a bullet ripping a path through his chest, but returned fire with a determined measure of accuracy. Renz was hit, but managed to pull the trigger again.

A shotgun blast roared in Mace's ears, as he felt a sharp pain in his gun arm that caused a total lost of feeling. Switching to his left hand, he fired back at Renz in a frenzy ... three – four – five shots. When his gun clicked on empty, Mace swayed sideways and sank to his knees.

It was surreal, staring through thick gunsmoke, its acrid smell in his nostrils. Mace could see Renz – still standing!

Then, his vision cleared and he realized Renz had backed up to the piano. He was not standing, but leaning against it, sitting on the keyboard protector. The eyes glaring at him were vacant and, as the final bit of life left his body, the man slid to the floor in a heap.

Wilcox looked at Mace, a curious expression on his face.

'Banyon?' he asked. 'Are you still alive?'

'Thought he'd never go down,' Mace found his voice. The words came out shaky, but at least he hadn't squeaked.

The sheriff snorted. 'Havelock didn't give me any trouble. You should have come armed like me. Ain't no need for fair play when you're wearing a badge.'

'I do believe you're right, Sheriff,' Mace said. 'I think my days of gunfighting are over.'

The doctor came in, a bit hesitant, but with his black medical bag. 'Is it safe?' he queried.'

Wilcox grinned. 'Yeah. Finally. Looks like Banyon won't be doing any more shooting. It ought to be a much safer town now.'

'I thought he hit me in the chest,' Mace explained to the doctor, 'but this bullet in my right shoulder caused me to lose all sensation.'

The doctor opened his shirt to examine the wounds. 'Dumb luck there,' he said. 'You have a crease between your ribs and arm – that would be the chest wound.' Then he felt around Mace's upper arm and shoulder. 'This other one will have to have some attention. Bullet is lodged against the bone.'

After looking at the two dead men, and assured Wilcox was uninjured, he took Mace to his office so he could remove the bullet.

Mace was sitting up, shirtless, while the doctor bandaged his right arm, when the front door was unceremoniously thrown open. Mercy came rushing into the room.

'Are you all right?' she cried. 'Wilcox said you were shot!'

'He'll live,' the doctor replied for him. 'If he holds still for me.'

She hurried over to them and looked closely at Mace. 'You hold still!' she ordered. 'Do like the doctor tells you.'

'I'm trying,' Mace said. 'I think this guy spends too much of his time working on mules. He's about the roughest sawbones I've ever been treated by.'

Just then, the doctor splashed his chest with alcohol. It felt like he'd ran a white-hot branding iron across the wound.

'Ye...ow!' Mace wailed. 'I was only kidding, Doc! You're the most gentle, tender-hearted medico I ever come across.'

Mercy laughed. 'Can I give him something for the pain, Doctor?'

'Be my guest,' he said.

Mace was dumbfounded, both at Mercy's action and her brass – she kissed him full on the lips. She pulled back after a moment and smiled.

'Better?'

He grinned provocatively. 'Uh, I got wounded twice. I need twice as much pain-killer.'

Mercy obliged and Mace decided being shot sometimes had its rewards.

END

ABOUT THE AUTHOR

Terrell L Bowers grew up playing cowboys, with his own horse and guns. His father got him to reading Westerns after he'd finished high school and, after a couple hundred titles, he began writing his own stories. Took him fifteen years before he found a receptive editor. Since that time, he has had over 40 titles published in the US and more than 30 titles published in the UK. He writes action, romance and humor in his stories, without the use of sex, gore or profanity. He is married, with two daughters and one grandchild.

Printed in Great Britain
by Amazon